I0675347

ANY <u>ONE</u> CAN DIE!

by

CHARLES NUETZEL

WRITING AS "GEORGE FREDRICS"

The Borgo Press
An Imprint of Wildside Press

MMVII

SECOND EDITION

CONTENTS

INTRODUCTION

Some stories simply surprise the author, many years later. Many times one will cringe in horror and wonder how it was possible to have written such tripe. This one was a surprise in a nice sort of way

It was originally published as *Appointment with Terror* by John Davidson, which wasn't at all a bad title, but later it was altered somewhat for its second run (after a normal translation in Europe) as the first half of *Consider Yourself Dead* by George Fredrics. Such a shady history to a suspense thriller.

Now, this time around, it is totally revised and expanded. But still the story of people caught in a horrible nightmare with a crazed killer who has just escaped from prison. A lifer with nothing to lose!

Sometimes a writer develops a villain who is totally without redeeming qualities, who one instantly learns to hate. I learned fast and was sucked into the story almost from the start, stunned by some of the antics that took place in that mountain cabin where a dozen people were snowed in and held captive by a sadistic madman. They did what he told them or died. In fact, chances were, they would all soon be dead! It was just a matter of when they died and in what order.

To some extend the location was, to me, kinda based on my personal exposure to Big Bear Lake and Lake Arrowhead, not far from where I live in Southern California. We don't get snow down here in the lowlands, which are, in reality, more like a kind of desert that runs right into the blue Pacific! Desert is all around Los Angeles, even if broken by low mountains that become richly green in winter and yellowish brown in summer. To see snow one has to seek the real higher mountains and there you have our "local" ski resorts and German style villa-type motels and country eateries. This is a lovely place to visit, and really a nice setting for this suspense novel.

It is somewhat interesting to revisit a story like this, even if it could turn into a nightmare of a different sort. Writers tend to either love or hate what they have set down on paper. Once printed it is too late to make changes. But not always! In this case I found myself quite pleased with what I discovered and even more pleased with how this revised version turned out.

—CHARLES NUETZEL
Thousand Oaks, California
July 2006

ACT ONE

ANY ONE CAN DIE! BY CHARLES NUETZEL

I.

CRIME MATES

Carl Anderson reluctantly moved from the woman on the bed at the first sound of a phone ringing. She squirmed, unhappily, looking at his lean muscular frame, eyes fairly devouring him. It was obvious that she resented the interruption.

"Sorry, babe!" he shrugged, grinning at the sight of her naked body lying stretched out there. She was a package! A real hungry lady.

He reached for the phone on the bed stand, saying into the receiver: "Hello?"

"This is Benny. Are you just about ready for the job?"

Carl looked at his watch and a stab of surprise and alarm rushed through him. Time had gone too fast in Helen's arms. He hadn't realized how late it was. 11:30—and they had the bank job to do at 1:00.

"Okay, I'll be ready. Coming up?"

"In a few minutes—if you can pull yourself away from that broad!" Benny's high-pitched voice laughed.

There was the sound of a click and then the phone went dead in his hands.

"Sorry!" he said, turning to Helen. "We'll have to continue this little thing later."

"What's with you? You get a girl all hot and hungry, then turn it off?" she complained, frowning at him and starting to sit up in bed.

He started getting dressed while saying: "You know the deal. Fun is one thing, but a million dollars is something else."

"Hardly a million, honey!" She stretched, letting him feast on her naked breasts. "Not a bank, Carl. Just a private PR firm...and they're loaded, big time in cash. So...be careful."

"Well, close enough! It's a 'bank job' to me and it'll clear each of us at least several hundred thousand bucks."

"Sure, I know that," she smiled, brushing her jet-black hair back off her forehead. "Wasn't I the one that told you about the deal? Wasn't I the woman working for them? What do you take me for? I might want your hard, male body—but not with all that money just waiting for us to take. Not on your life, big-daddy!" She stood, smiled, and then moved close, pulling herself against him.

They kissed long and hard. Then she moved away. "You sure that your brother won't be up at the cabin?"

"Who's sure about anything? But one thing I do know, Noel don't go up to it much."

"Okay..." she sighed. "Just so we don't have company up there. That's all I say!"

"I can't promise nothing but a safe hideout—I couldn't say anything to Noel—'cause he don't even know I broke jail. Let him know that and he'd turn me in. And real fast. We haven't had much use for one another for years."

"So, get ready," she told him, "Benny should be here any minute—shouldn't he?"

"Sure thing, babe...and I'll bet he'll be here sooner than he told me. He's nervous as hell!"

"That's bad—I'm afraid, dear," she said, seriously. "He's too nervous. He could queer the whole thing if some cop came along. He's gun happy!"

"You leave him to me."

"Okay, okay. You see that nothing happens. The watchman doesn't make the rounds until later but it'll be a close thing..."

"Right!"

"The timer I set for 1:15 AM!"

"I know. I know. You told me a hundred times."

10

"Don't get mad! Details are important!" she cried, heatedly. "And, anyway, I'm the one hurting for that hard bod of yours!" She smiled quickly. "You know...all that we were doing! Can't wait to give you a real pick me up, later."

"Okay...Okay!"

"Okay!" she half screamed. "It's my idea—the whole thing! So don't get so hot around the collar! Just keep it hot...down there, where it counts, luv!"

They both laughed, then hurriedly dressed.

There was a knock on the door and both of them turned in that direction at once as if the FBI were about to break in and arrest them.

"Who is it?"

"Benny!" a thin voice answered them through the paneling. "Who else?"

"Okay—we'll be right there!" Carl announced, looking at himself in the mirror, straightening his tie and then turning toward Helen. "Ready?"

She smiled, leaning close and kissing his cheek.

"Okay—then," he said, "let's get the show on the road!"

Any <u>One</u> Can Die! by Charles Nuetzel

II.

SECOND PARTY

In another town several hours earlier, there was a party taking place. Gene Bates was looking at the woman who was sitting on the sofa. This was his "blind date" for the evening. For a long moment he wondered what he was doing at such a party. She was bleach blonde. Her lips were large and sensuous, body full, voluptuous. The kind of woman who needed a man more than she needed food or drink. Or that's the image she brazenly offered up. But he hated being alone.

Thoughtfully he dropped his eyes down at the glass in his hands. A strong highball, whose strength was already beginning to hit him. He would need to be loaded to take this lady on. She simply wasn't his type. She was being dumped on him because he was lonely and frustrated. "You need a hot lady!" Ray had told him. "Let you forget Ms Chill!"

Patricia Taylor! She wasn't really that way. Not really Ms Chill at all! She was one of those "nice" ladies. He'd played it very proper with her. And she had run away from him because she was afraid of marriage. And that was why he was here tonight. He had to run, too. But his reasons were a little different than Pat's. He had been running for a long time. Running from himself and the fact that he had no real direction in life—no goal. Until he met Pat. Then things had changed. He had wanted to marry Pat and have kids. So now where was he? Right back where he had started. Alone. And it hurt like an open wound after a couple of weeks agonizing over their separation.

"What's with you, pal?" Ray Nicholas cried, patting Gene on the shoulder and pushing him forward. "You don't have to be bashful with Rena!"

Gene shook his head slowly and then took a long swallow of his drink. He had to meet the lady, sometime— and the sooner the better.

"Play her right," Ray whispered in his ear as they moved through the crowded room. "She'll drop you like a hot potato if you don't look promising. After a while we'll head for the apartment." Ray's boyish face broke into a broad smile as they approached the woman that had been invited to the party for Gene.

"Hello there, doll!" Ray greeted.

She looked up and smiled. "Hi, I was hoping you'd be at the party."

"Have a friend here I told you about." Ray indicated Gene.

The girl just looked at Gene, and smiled.

"Rena Green," Ray introduced, "this is Gene Bates."

That was the extent of the introduction, because just then a tall red head stepped up to Ray and took his arm. "Come on—don't wanna be alone!"

"Okay, okay, Junie." He turned to Gene. "Gotta go, you see how it is."

For a long moment Gene stood there looking at the blonde, not knowing what to say. It was one of those awkward situations when there just wasn't really anything to say. They were just two strangers being thrown together for one purpose: a shack-up one night stand; and with no silly games about it.

Finally she half smiled, as if trying to force herself to be polite.

"Well, what now?" she asked, not standing, just looking strangely into his eyes.

Gene held down a helpless shrug. He just wasn't used to this kind of game. Gene had always taken time with his women. To him a lot of romancing preceded intimacy. One night stands weren't his style—normally, anyway.

"Well," he finally said, forcing himself to begin the

14

game, "How about a drink?"

Rena nodded and then stood.

"Why not?—nothing like a drink to get things moving," she announced brightly, gliding up beside him. She stood there, very close, boldly saying without words that she was his for the taking.

The way she used her body as she walked had all the elements of a cat stalking her mate. Her hand slid around his arm and her fingers seemed to tighten a little. "Lead on, Mr. Gene Bates!"

They moved across the crowded room toward the large bar in the corner. This was one of the weekly parties that a group of rich guys put on. Free spirited women, a bit of booze, drugs and a lot of sex being tossed around for the easy taking. This was Ray Nicholas' playing field, into which Gene was being quickly introduced. The only thing was that Gene didn't have the money to really keep up with such a rich crowd—Ray did, and Ray was one of his best buddies. They had met in the service and ever since then one time or another they'd gotten together. The relationship had always been awkward for Gene, because Ray always had some "broad" or "chick" or "whore" clutching eagerly at his arm, and Gene had most of the time been a loner. But now things were going to change; starting with tonight and this bleach blonde slut named Rena Green. No more romantic idealism; no more silly complications. Just enjoy life, like Ray had insisted. Enjoy this blonde bombshell of a lady who was without question more than willing to enjoy a lively date with a stranger—one that ended up with a good-morning hug or more.

The feel of her suggested that Rena was one lush package, who enjoyed a man, and not about to hide those feelings behind foolish "hands off" prudishness. In fact, as Ray had warned: it was look and touch all you want! Or else, goodbye, Gene!

They stepped up to the bar and Gene walked around the small counter.

"What'll it be?" he asked, trying to make his voice sound light and breezy.

"Anything, anything at all!" she told him, giving him

the once-over for the first time. The way her greenish colored eyes swept up and down his body made a heated tingle run across his spine. No doubt about her sensuality, and sexual appeal. Any man would find her quite a delicious snack to hungrily devour.

Nervously he took the glass he had been carrying in his hand, and raised it to his lips. The face of Pat Taylor formed in his mind. Her delicate figure, attractive and with a lot of sex appeal—but not in the raw animal way that Rena displayed herself. Pat's breasts weren't as large nor had they ever been as exposed as Rena's now were. Slowly her figure faded out and in its place the image of Rena voluptuous form returned.

She was sitting there on the stool, looking at him with a strange expression on her face.

"What's wrong?" she asked.

"What?"

"You been standing there for several minutes—looking right through me! It gives me the creeps!"

"Sorry." He dropped his eyes to the bar where all the bottles were sitting, just waiting for him to start mixing any kind of drink he desired. "You want to fly?"

"Sure, why not? But...none of the hard stuff..." She laughed a bit brazenly. "I mean...of course...liquor, only. Never went for any nose-sniffing stuff."

He glanced at her. "That's a strange way of putting it."

"I don't drive to drugs, honey. A man, well, that's just fine with me. I want to keep a clear head."

"That makes the two of us. No drugs is my theme. But you, I would have thought otherwise."

"Oh? Really?" She sounded a bit miffed. "Why would you think that? I'm just a lady who enjoys a good man! Anything wrong with that?"

He managed a grin, but said nothing.

She watched as he reached for gin, vodka and rum. A jigger of each went into two glasses. Then he took the coke bottle and filled the glasses. Handing her one he started gulping on his own.

"Hold on, Gene-boy! You don't want to pass out on

16

this baby!" she told him, taking hold of his wrist and pulling the glass away from his lips. "I want more than just a drunk on my hands. If you get my meaning! Drinks might warm you a little, but too many melt you down, fast. Let me do the warming part! You'll enjoy it far better. I promise."

His eyes met hers for a moment and then dropped downwards to where her dress opened at the front offering a full view of her full breasts that swelled against the clothing.

"I've been told you're a man who could enjoy a woman like me. So give yourself a break!" Her voice was strangely level, surprisingly frank. "A drunk man can't make a girl very happy! And you seem like a nice guy, who could enjoy a bit of distraction with somebody who isn't complicated. That's what we all come here for. A bit of escape from the daily routine of surviving! That can be tough on all of us, Gene."

She was right, of course. Ray was right.

Escape was the key word. Escape by running to a woman like her. Normally it would have been a dive into a bottle to escape any conscious awareness of the hurt that he was still feeling. Escape from the memory of Pat...and the plans he had made for the two of them.

"Sure baby...why get drunk when I have you? Right?" The line rolled off his tongue as if he had been used to handing it out; like he did it in the very course of breathing.

He moved around the bar and sat on the bar stool next to Rena. Maybe it would be fun escaping into the very depths of this voluptuously shaped lady.

"Tell me something about yourself," he suggested, his hand squeezing her fingers.

Her leg touched his. "Well, there isn't much to say—really. I just work at a factory during the day, and go out in the evening. That's about it."

"There must be something."

"No—really. You see all there is to see of me. Quite frankly, I have the looks ... and I kinda like living on the wild side, if you know what I mean."

That sentence seemed to sum up her whole existence; it also said something about her mental make-up—she was honest with herself and not afraid to admit the truth. That was at least one point in her favor. In fact, he was feeling a little bit better about the woman; she was, actually, rather nice.

"How about yourself?" she asked.

"Just bumming around…I suppose. Used to work on a newspaper—now just living with Ray. Trying to decide what to do next."

"Sounds pretty nice, not having to worry about bills or anything," she told him, reaching her arm around his neck.

Gene downed a large part of his drink, because the light heady effects were beginning to wear off and that was one thing that he didn't want to happen.

She reached out and took hold of his glass. "You don't need that, now do you? Not with me."

He let her take the drink from him, sit it on the bar.

The woman was quite different from what he'd expected.

"Say," she said, smiling brightly, "Why don't we do a little dancing?"

"No music!"

"That's nothing. There's a CD player in the den—and I know our host won't mind."

Gene glanced at his drink, but let it stay there on the bar, next to hers.

They moved toward a small room, weaving in and out of the group of people. As they reached the doorway to the den, they bumped into Ray and his girl friend.

"Say," Ray greeted, smiling drunkenly, "How're you doing?"

"Fine—just fine," he told his friend.

"Want to cut out?"

Rena moved closer to Gene and pressed her hip against his. "Let's! We can dance…or whatever…elsewhere!"

18

III.

THE THIRD ELEMENT

Patricia Taylor was sitting in a bar, lonely and confused. It had been several weeks since she had last seen Gene Bates, and she couldn't really get him out of her mind. There had been a bond which was very strong between the two of them, and that was one thing which she couldn't mentally destroy or forget, no matter how hard she tried.

Love! she thought, *it was one sickening thing that got into your blood and couldn't get out—or wouldn't.*

But the trouble with Gene had been that he was just too nice a guy—and a little too confused as to what he wanted to be. That had been one of the reasons she had been afraid to continue things with him. She wanted something else in life—something that would give her adventure and excitement. The idea of settling down and having children frightened her.

She gulped the drink in her hand and then motioned the cocktail waitress over. "Another—and this time make it a double!"

The girl went away with a surprised expression on her face. But Pat didn't really care; she didn't care what anybody thought about her drinking so much.

She'd made a mistake about running out on Gene— that much she knew. They had never really connected honestly. Instead of being like two people desperately in love, they had been purely practical. "We must be honest with each other. After all, we aren't school kids anymore!" they

19

had said over and over to each other. Gene thought he wanted love and romance and marriage and kids. And she didn't want to do anything but have a ball and live it up for a little longer, before she was too old to really enjoy it. Yet something had stopped her from telling him that, nor even implying her real desires.

With another man it might have been possible to leap into a hot affair—be swept off her feet. But with Gene she'd hesitated. What if such an offer would shock him? Would he dump her, cold. She'd heard that some men were like that. For some reason she hadn't wanted to kill the relationship on that level. So, instead, she'd let it be cut off because he wanted marriage—and she'd run from him.

What a damned fool I am.

So here she was, alone and by herself in a saloon, "really living it up!" Getting drunk—alone! And she wasn't a heavy drinker!

The cocktail waitress returned and placed the double highball in front of Pat, and then left.

She should have gone out with her boss this evening. Noel Anderson: large, slightly heavy, and a bit of a rake. The only thing wrong with Noel was that he was married—separated from his wife and all that—but married.

She didn't believe in going out with a married man, separated or not. She didn't believe in going out with her boss, single or otherwise. And she didn't believe in being by herself on Saturday night, either. Several weeks alone had been enough!

Gripping the glass tightly, she raised it to her lips and took several large swallows. The liquor reached her head with a whirling excitement. She was beginning to feel a little better—and a little happier.

Just then a good-looking young man stepped up to her table and coughed. She looked at him for a moment, wondering what he was doing standing there so awkwardly.

"Pardon me, but you look kinda lonely."

"Oh?" she managed. "It shows?"

"A little, I suppose. Want company?"

She studied him carefully. He wasn't bad looker. Obviously out to connect with a woman.

20

"Could I buy you a drink?" He smiled slightly, but his eyes seemed to be a little fearful, as if afraid she might turn him down and he wouldn't know how to handle it.

She wanted to send him packing. She was lonely and she did want company. And, quite frankly, she didn't give a damned! She'd blown it with Gene by being too careful. She claimed to want the wild life; a little adventure. Now here she must start!

"That would be nice," she told him, offering the chair on the other side of the table. But he took the one next to her.

She just nodded, drank down her highball and indicated that her glass was empty.

The man called over the cocktail waitress. "Another for the lady, and one of the same for me."

They sat for a long time without saying anything. Pat was beginning to get nervous and wishing that she hadn't taken up the offer of a free drink. She wondered what Gene was doing tonight. The drinks came, and before the cocktail waitress had even left, she had half downed hers and ordered another.

The world seemed to spin dangerously; everything took on a cloudy glow. The music in the background seemed more centered in her mental focus than before. Nervously she took out a cigarette from her purse and the man lighted it for her. Normally she didn't smoke, but since the break up with Gene she'd been doing a lot of foolish things.

Neither of them had said much for the last few minutes. He was looking carefully at her, as if trying to figure the best approach to pick her up. It made her uncomfortable, but in a way it seemed to send a thrill shooting through her to think that a man would be so obviously interested.

The idea of wanting to be needed—sexually—caused her to be slightly excited. To be swept up in a man's arms, literally off her feet, and taken away where he could overpower all her silly little efforts to resist seemed such a wonderful temptation. Right from some romantic historical novel! "Raped" of all resistance, so it wouldn't "really" be her fault! Well, she told herself, it wasn't anything like rape, but it could be simply being swept away by an overpowering, deliciously attractive, strong male who was motivated by such desire for her that she'd be overwhelmed and simply lost in the ecstatic pleasure of his love-making. So the story went. A Knight to spend a deliciously lovely night of passion with, an instant simple escape. A dream without any long-lasting ties, such as marriage vows, children, settling down before she had even lived.

She sipped the highball, much faster than she realized. Her mind was beginning to race madly, trying to think of some way she could handle the situation.

She felt his hand reach for hers. A tingling excitement rushed through her.

"You sure make a man want to take you someplace... private..." he was saying in a husky voice. "How about it? Want to stay here? Or...we could..."

His voice trailed off as he watched the expression on her face.

This was the moment of decision. She either let him lead her away to his place, her place or some seedy motel room.

What was she doing? Getting drunk with a stranger.

Planning a quickie one night stand!

She must be out of her mind!

Confused. And lonely. And angry with herself. But quite nuts! This wasn't what she wanted!

This wasn't some dream; it was a nightmare in the making!

Nervously she looked at the glass and then angrily slammed it down on the table, stood and then without even looking at the man ran from the saloon. Shaking, she climbed into her car and started the engine, put it into gear and directed it down the street toward her apartment. Through the drunken fog and the emotional terror of her own physical desires, she didn't realize how fast she was traveling or how dangerously.

Only one thought was rushing madly through her brain:

She had come too close to giving into impulse. For a brief moment she had almost decided to play along with the man. The sound of a siren disturbed her thoughts. At first she couldn't get the direction of the screaming focused in her mind. Then finally she heard that it was directly behind her—then she saw the flashing red light.

Police.

Pat brought the car to a stop and a moment later the policeman was standing at the door next to her.

"What's the difficulty, lady? Where you going in such a hurry?"

She tried to focus her eyes on his face, but it was almost impossible.

"I don't know what I've done, officer," she said in evenly spaced words and a controlled tone of voice.

"Been drinking?"

"Why, officer..." just then she hiccupped. "Please, officer, I gotta get home."

"That's what they all say. I'll get Frank to follow us on in. Move over and I'll drive."

"I really don't see what all the fuss is all about!" she cried heatedly, slurring her words for the first time.

"Let the judge decide that, tomorrow, after you've had a chance to sober up a little, miss."

ANY ONE CAN DIE! BY CHARLES NUETZEL

IV.

THE KILL

Carl Anderson moved in the shadows of the bank, nervously gripping the gun in his hands. He knew that it was only a matter of seconds before the vault timer went off, and the huge door would slide open before his eyes.

Anxiously he looked at the slender man beside him. Benny's eyes were wide and bright. They looked in Carl's direction for a moment and a weak grin spread across his weak lips.

"Any second," he whispered. "This is a dream. You're squeeze is smart. She sure set things up smart. You're lucky. Just so nobody discovers us!"

There was the sound of a light click and then the two of them moved forward and Carl opened the vault. In a few moments they would be rich and heading up to his brother's mountain cabin. That would be a great place to hide out. Nobody to bother them; nothing. Then they'd stay there in safety until the whole scare blew over.

Quickly he opened the gunnysack and silently motioned to Benny to start filling it with all that green fortune which would set them up for the rest of their lives.

Millions! Well, maybe not that much. But thousands, hundreds of thousands, at the very least!

Carl was just folding the large gunnysack over the tightly packed bundle of bills that had forcefully been pushed into it, when the voice of the night watchman suddenly broke into the darkness and silence.

"What's going on here?" were the explosive words.

Benny turned, a frightened expression squeezing his features with terror.

Slowly, Carl moved in the direction of the threatening voice. For a moment he couldn't see beyond the glowing beam of the flashlight which was held by the faceless man in the darkness beyond.

"Just stay where you are, and don't move!" the man ordered in a tight, set voice. "I think maybe the police might want to be talking to you two." The casual surliness in the man's words sent a chill of sickness rippling through Carl. Then his mind started to work like a speeding, well-oiled machine.

He couldn't let the man call the police. If the law got to him again it would be the end of his activities for good—life in prison or...the electric chair. His whole survival depended on getting through this caper safe. The money would set him up for a life of ease in some country in South America; that was the only reason he had gone for it. He'd need money so that he could disappear from the country.

"Benny, don't!" he shouted in terror, suddenly turning to the smaller man standing quietly frozen in terror at his side.

The words and his abrupt action got the reaction he had hoped for. The night watchman's flashlight turned toward Benny and his voice jabbed through the air. "Freeze!"

"Don't," Carl shouted again, "Put the gun away!"

The weaponless man cringed back in terror as the watchman's gun blazed in the semi-darkness; then he jerked backwards as if hit by a giant hand. Blood oozed from his chest as a moan of agony burst from his lips.

Then there was a second explosive shot as the gun which had leaped into Carl's hand flamed from the barrel.

Carl's finger squeezed again and again, and a thin grin of pleasure and raw excitement spread across his features as he saw the watchman smash backwards, stumble, and jerk with each impact of the bullets as they ripped through his stomach. A groan of agonized pain and terror cried out from his lips as they became red with blood.

Carl moved forward and kicked the man's face. Then

26

he smashed downwards into the watchman's stomach; it was wasted effort, because the man was already dead, but that didn't seem to bother him in the least—or lessen the grin of satisfaction.

Finally he turned toward his bleeding friend, who was lying on the floor of the vault, holding his hands over a bloody blotch on his chest.

"God—God, oh God, Carl—I'm shot..."

Carl leaned over his friend. "Can you move?"

The man just shook his head from side to side, pain showing on his twisted features. "No—no..."

Without so much as changing expression, Carl pointed the gun toward Benny and squeezed the trigger. Then he turned and gathered up the gunny-sack of money and, lifting it over his shoulders, moved toward the door. A moment later he stepped into the waiting car.

"Get going!" was his only command.

ANY <u>ONE</u> CAN DIE! BY CHARLES NUETZEL

V.

ESCAPE ROUTE ONE

Carl Anderson and Helen had been driving for a long time before she said anything to him. Finally she turned and looked at Carl, her face tense with worry and concern.

"What happened to Benny?" she demanded in a clipped tone of voice, looking back at the road.

"Got killed," he told her, taking a cigarette and lighting it.

"How'd it happen?"

"The night watchman turned up. Things got pretty thick and it was necessary to have a shoot out."

"But you said that he didn't have a gun—" she pointed out, gripping the wheel tighter.

"He didn't. But the watchman thought he did."

"Strange."

"Get off my back. I told you what happened. That's all there is to it!"

"So—you shot the man?"

"Had to. Couldn't leave any witnesses."

"Poor Benny."

"Hell, he was just a..." Carl forced his voice to fade out. He didn't dare let Helen know exactly what had really happened. He couldn't let her know that it had been necessary for him to finish off Benny because the man didn't have a chance of coming with them, and he couldn't afford to leave any witnesses behind to let the police know where he was heading, or who had done the job.

No witnesses and there would be no chance of being caught. It was a clean job—with no hitches; unless the death of Benny could be called a hitch.

"Anyway—what's the beef? We just got that much more for ourselves, baby!"

The look on her face as she turned toward him caused Carl to add: "What I mean is—what's done is done. We can't do nothing about that. Benny's dead, and nothing we might have wanted differently can change that fact. So let's look in the happy side of things. More money."

"So he's dead!" Her voice sounded faraway and strangely flat. For a moment longer she looked at him and then back at the road.

They didn't say anything for a long time and then suddenly there was an explosive sound as one of the tires burst flat.

Frantically Helen twisted the wheel and the car whipped around, jumped into the ditch alongside the road and then plunged forward toward a large tree.

Carl jumped into action, forcefully grabbing the wheel and jerking it powerfully from the woman's control.

"Goddamn!" was his only word as he finally managed to just miss crashing into the tree and instead, slid along the ditch.

There was the sound of another blow-out and the car finally came to a grinding stop, sending both passengers forward against the windshield.

For a long time neither of them moved. Then finally Helen stirred and slowly sat up.

Her eyes showed a blank dazed look, as if she were trying to remember what had happened; then she looked around her and saw Carl's head limp on the windshield.

Frantically she pulled him back, laying his head on the seat. Her head went to his chest and then her features relaxed.

"Thank God!" she half sobbed, sitting up. "Thank God you're alive."

VI.

BROTHER NOEL

Pat Taylor sat in the car next to her boss, Noel Anderson. It was still dark outside, even though it was as near dawn as it could get without the sun actually being visible or its light brightening the eastern horizon.

"I feel terrible, Mr. Anderson," she said as he drove the car away from the police station.

"Think nothing of it. After all, if a girl can't turn to her friends for help, then who can she look to? The only thing is I don't see how you got yourself into such a mess."

She didn't say anything because suddenly she felt guilty about the whole thing. She didn't want to admit that she'd been in a bar alone and let a man buy her a couple of drinks—and then walked out on him. At least, she didn't want to let Noel Anderson know—not after having refused to go out with him that evening.

"You were lucky that they didn't throw you in jail and then throw away the key!" Noel said, brushing his graying hair back off his forehead. "They had a list of charges...speeding, drunken driving, and running several stoplights." His voice was not scolding—but amazed. "It's just a good thing that the judge knows me—otherwise you'd be cooling yourself off in jail for a couple of days! And that's for sure!"

"Let's not talk about it, please, Mr. Anderson," she pleaded.

"Noel...not Mr. Anderson. How many times do I have

to remind you?"

"Okay, Mr.—I mean Noel," she smiled half sadly. Her head was beginning to react from the drinks' after effects. A throbbing ache. But it wasn't hard to smile at Noel; he'd been so kind about waking up in the middle of the night to get her out of the police station. At first she had only reacted—calling the first person that came to mind, and that had been Noel Anderson. And the next thing she knew he was getting her out. No fuss, no difficulties about it. Just "come along, everything is taken care of," and then walking through the police station and to his car.

No, it was easy enough to smile at Noel Anderson. Maybe she had been foolish in originally turning down his offer to take her someplace. So he was married—after all, he was separated from his wife. And he had a right to live his life the way he wished to, now. And then, really, what was wrong with going out with your boss? It might even be good for business.

She decided to take him up on the next offer of a date—if he ever asked her again.

Finally they pulled up in front of a restaurant. "Hungry?" he asked.

The suggestion of food brought hunger pangs. She nodded, and the two of them walked in. It was the first time they had really been alone together. They seated themselves and then after reading the menus and ordering they looked at each other for a long time without saying anything. Then finally he smiled and shook his head from side to side. "I don't know about you. How you can ever be safe all by yourself. You get in the damndest fixes."

"I feel so ... embarrassed. This is the first time I've ever...well... you know!"

"Well, at least it looks like I got to take you out after all."

She nodded.

"I'm glad you called me."

"It was horrible of me—wasn't it?"

"No—no! not at all. In fact, I'm quite flattered. You're the first female who has turned to me for help in a long time. My wife never seemed to think I was able to give

34

her any help—she...well that's another subject!"

Pat just smiled, but said nothing. For some reason she really didn't know what to say. Maybe it was the hangover.

The food came and they ate in silence. Afterwards, just talking about generalities, they sipped coffee. It was getting light out and Noel looked at his watch. "Pretty near work time..." then his voice broke off, embarrassed. "I forgot—this is Sunday."

She laughed and then nodded her head. "You had me fooled for a moment. I felt those Monday blues in the middle of my stomach. Or maybe that was just the hangover."

"You have anything planned for today?" he asked, blurting it out as if he had been holding it back for several moments and finally had not been able to keep it in any longer.

The question left her slightly surprised. She hadn't expected it. She just looked at him and then down at the cup of coffee in her hands.

"I mean...this afternoon! You'll be needing some sleep."

"Not really," she said, making up her mind. "And I don't have anything planned at all."

"Great! Then!"

They sat, saying nothing for a few moments, and then his face brightened. "Say, how would you like to go up to the mountains? I have a cabin there—and we could...well?"

She thought that over. The mountains would be nice. But it could also make for an awkward situation. In his cabin, alone, she had no idea what might take place. Then she realized what a stuffy little child she was being. Noel wouldn't do anything that she wouldn't want him to do. That was one thing she could say for him: he was a gentleman. "Why not?"

"It'll be a wonderful drive and I know you'll like the lake. You have a bathing suit?" He was bubbling and suddenly he seemed to realize it. "I'm sorry. But I've been wanting to take you out for a long time—as you know. Please. Forgive me?"

"What for? For being nice and honest? Come on—let's get over to my place, so that I can change and get a few things."

"Great idea!" He motioned the waitress over and paid the bill.

As the two of them got into the car she couldn't help feeling a slight affection for Noel; he was so much like a little boy. A little boy at Christmas time who has been given a very special gift that he'd been waiting for, for a long time.

He looked at her for a second and then smiled. He started the engine, and in a few moments they were driving towards her apartment.

VII.

ESCAPE ROUTE TWO

Helen had two choices: to use her cell to call the hospital, or she could flag down a car and hold up the driver. It was the latter that she decided on. If nothing else, Helen was a practical woman.

Taking the gun from Carl's pocket and putting it in her own, she got out on the road. A car had to come by some time or other, even on such a lonely road such as this.

She waited for a long time; for what seemed hours—but in reality was only about fifteen minutes. Then a car came roaring by. It didn't stop.

A few minutes later another car came—but it was going the wrong way. It stopped. A man's head looked out.

"Can I help you, miss?" The voice was old sounding and slightly shaking.

"I think you can," she said, taking the gun from her pocket and pointing it at the graying and lined face.

The graying face turned white as it focused on the gun in Helen's hands.

"Get out, old man," she demanded, motioning with the gun. "I need a little help with a hurt man here."

In a few moments he was helping her lift Carl carefully from her car and moving him over to his own.

"Thanks a lot," she said, sitting behind the wheel, "I don't think you'll be...needing this any more!" Then she broke off and quickly got out of the car and moved to her own. In seconds she had the huge gunnysack transferred into the old man's car. She started the engine, then turned the car around and headed in the direction they had been driving before the blowouts, leaving the old man standing in the road.

She turned and looked at Carl, a worried expression clouding her face.

She hoped he'd come to before long. If not she'd have to take him to a doctor—and that was dangerous; much too dangerous. The only other alternative would be to let him die.

She thought of the money taken from the safe. All for her if he died.

That was, strangely enough, not what Helen wanted.

Wake up, you no good slob! she cried mentally. *Oh, wake up!*

VIII.

RENA

When morning came, Gene Bates had angry emotional pangs. He woke up with a hangover to begin with; then he remembered the woman lying in bed next to him. That's when he felt the inner stab of guilt.

Pure animal passions—and nothing more. Raw, wild, overwhelming. Sure. The woman had been one bundle of free-giving sex, no holds barred.

He remembered how she had come at him almost the moment they were alone in the room. And her lips were open wide as the crushed up under his. She literally pressed his hands into her breasts. Clothing had disappeared in a flash of movement mixed with hot kisses and clawing caresses. She was quite intense and full of raw energy that smothered his mind of any thoughts other than possessing her body. He remembered her breasts under his lips, and later the feel of her gripping tightly to him as she arched up to meet every pounding thrust of their bodies hammered wildly at one another.

Sharp visions, yet scattered in incomplete chunks. His head hurt.

Slowly he stood and walked from the room. He wanted to be alone for a few moments. Alone to think things out; to try to figure just what kind of damned fool he was.

Quickly he got dressed and then after having a cup of coffee and smoking a couple of cigarettes he walked out of the apartment he now shared with Ray and down to the street below.

Rena had been really something last night. He had to admit that. All sexual energy, directly furious at consuming the man in her arms. Guilt stabbed at him. Pat's image formed in his mind. Why did she have to always pop up? That was the trouble; he couldn't forget her. And that was why he had gone to Ray in the first place and asked about living with him for a while and being introduced to a woman like Rena.

He turned around and started back in the direction of the apartment. A few moments later he was walking into the front room. Ray and his girl and Rena were sitting at the breakfast table with robes wrapped loosely around them.

"Hi, what in the world happened to you?" Ray asked, looking in his direction.

"Just took a walk," was Gene's only reply.

"Well, come on over and join us. We were fixing eggs and the works," Rena cried in a cheery voice.

He sat and the four of them carried on a conversation that finally shifted to what they planned on doing that afternoon. Together.

"The beach?" Rena suggested, brightly. In some ways she actually seemed quite nice.

"How about the desert?" Ray's girl suggested.

"No, June, it'll be too damn hot!" Ray exclaimed.

"Then the beach?" Rena asked again, winking at Gene as if sharing some private, intimate secret—or promise. It was difficult not to kinda like her, in a way. She might be a bit too much, but, on the other hand, seemed so warm and friendly.

"We can always go to the beach," June cried.

Gene suddenly got a good idea. "The mountains. There might be snow up there and I haven't been skiing for years."

Everybody jumped at the idea.

"We can pack a lunch—" Rena suggested, springing to her feet, just like a little girl. There was a strange and appealing childlike counterpoint to her raw sexual energy, and image, which was hardly subdued under the loosely fitting robe, so open at the top that her naked breasts were peaking

40

IX.

THE CABIN

The drive up to the mountains was a relaxing and exciting thing to Pat. It was something new to be doing on a long weekend—or at least it all seemed new to her, because it had been such a long time since she'd been to a mountain lake.

They had checked the weather reports and discovered that it had snowed the night before, so they had brought their ski clothes. It turned out that Noel Anderson was a ski fan, too, and they were both excited about the idea of being able to have a little winter sport.

But there was more than just this response to the idea of going to the mountains; the unexpectedness of their plans was almost unnerving. The impulsive brought to life! Yes. On impulse without second thoughts. Maybe she could learn to breath freely, and not be confined to such a restricted life-style. Considering the beginning of the weekend, her life had been altered. One moment she was arrested and the next eating breakfast and after that the accepting the invite to go to the mountains with Noel.

It had been necessary to put chains on the tires long before they reached their destination, for the snow was thick and heavy, quite low on the mountains. The chilly air left their cheeks red, and Pat's body felt alive and eager to get out in the snow. After that they didn't leave the car until Noel had pulled up into the driveway of his large mountain cabin. It was a nice, lovely wood framed structure, with a

43

high pointed ceiling, covered in snow. A very rustic, homey site. And nicely isolated.

"Well, here we are, at last!" He announced, turning off the engine and stepping out of the car. After a moment he was on her side, opening the door and helping her out.

She felt her heart beat faster and faster as she stepped out of the car and walked across the snow and finally up to the cabin porch. It had taken all the control she had to keep from stooping down and grabbing a handful of white snow. But she realized that this wasn't the time—yet. They would have all day before they had to leave for town again. All day in the snow. It had only been a three hour drive to his cabin and it was still quite early in the morning.

Noel opened the cabin door and directed Pat in.

She was surprised by the modern furnishing of the place. She had expected to find a rustic style, but instead she found a completely modern layout. Only the fireplace was semi-rustic, in stone.

"How beautiful!" she exclaimed, making a circle of the room. "You really have a place here!"

"Oh, it's not so bad. Some people think it's rather odd the way I've furnished it. But I like it. Come on along, and I'll show you the rest."

He took her hand and led her around the large cabin. There were two bedrooms and a large kitchen and the living room. In the living room was a small home bar, and Noel finally brought an end of his tour before it.

"How about one?" he suggested, indicating the large supply of liquor he had stocked in a cabinet on the wall in back of the bar.

She thought seriously for a moment, her lips pursing. Then she shrugged her shoulders. "I guess it won't hurt, at that. After all, they say the best thing after a big drink-night is a drink! But something light."

"Sure thing, Pat. Sure thing!" Noel exclaimed starting to mix a gin & tonic. After a second or so he handed her one.

"To us! And a wonderful day!" he saluted, taking a strong swallow of his drink.

She lifted her glass to her lips and sipped carefully. The drink tasted good, but she refused to down it too fast.

44

Not after last night and what almost happened to her with a stranger. She would have to be careful this evening because Noel wasn't a stranger, and he had a certain amount of animal appeal that most women found delicious.

"Believe me, Pat, I couldn't be happier having you up here with me. A man gets so tired of coming to a place like this all alone. And I guess I've been needing a little fun ... well, companionship with a woman."

She didn't quite know how to take that last line, but decided to smile and accept it at face value. She only hoped that he didn't try anything too fast or demanding; it would ruin everything for her. And there was a good chance it would make her lose her job. Suddenly she experienced doubts about having come here with him. Maybe it had been a mistake. Could she possibly keep him at arm's length? Did she want to? Should she want to?

After the drink, Noel suggested that they might as well change into their ski clothes and get the show on the road.

Pat didn't need a second invitation—in fact she could hardly wait until they were gliding down some snowy slope.

Twenty minutes later they were back in the car, driving toward the ski lift. The drink that Pat had had was still lightly coursing through her veins, making her whole body feel warm. Things felt different, now; more relaxed.

"This is the most fun I've had for a long time!" she told him, moving closer to Noel. "Thanks for asking me!"

"Think nothing of it—the pleasure is all mine!"

But she was thinking a lot about it. The trip had been a very good idea—for other reasons than the ones she might tell Noel. It was already beginning to help her forget the hard lump that was eating through her whenever she thought of Gene Bates. The silly thing was that it had been several weeks since they had broken up—and she couldn't get him out of her mind. Maybe it was because she had been the one who walked out—and she knew deep down that if she wanted to, she could return. She could call Gene up and start all over. But that was one thing that she had promised herself she wouldn't do.

So now she was up in the mountains with Noel

45

Anderson for one purpose and one purpose alone: To start doing something more than just moping around her apartment all by herself, like she'd been doing the last few weeks. She surely needed something to do to change her life in a better way; give it some direction and purpose.

Having an affair with a married man? she wondered. *Are you kidding yourself?*

Well, okay, he was free, kinda. Getting a divorce. So maybe she could give him a break. And herself, as well.

She decided to stop fussing around about it all and try to simply enjoy whatever happened—as long as it seemed right at that moment.

She needed a fresh outlook on life; a fresh beginning.

And this was as good a start as she could think of. She had made her decision when he'd asked her to come here with him.

So, lady, stop quibbling! Live for the moment!

That was why she had gone with Noel—and she had better make the best of it. She was supposed to be enjoying herself—and damn it all, she would!

ACT THREE

ANY ONE CAN DIE! BY CHARLES NUETZEL

X.

THE LODGE

Not far from where Noel parked his car near the ski-lift, Ray Nicholas swung up the main road to the huge lodge which served as the main headquarters for most of the tourists and skiers.

"Well, here we are, gang!" he cried, stepping from the car.

A few moments later Gene followed Rena into the large lodge reception room. There was a roaring fire in the corner, huge and surrounded by stone blocks in the shape of a huge fireplace. Several people were standing around it, warming themselves.

"Boy, it's cold!" June cried, rushing for the fireplace. "I need a little heating!"

Rena followed and Ray and Gene went to the front desk.

"What can I do for you?" the smallish clerk asked, smiling professionally at them.

"Two doubles," Ray instructed the man, "with a view!"

They registered and took the keys, then motioned the women to follow them.

"We'll take care of the luggage later," Ray said.

"Why not now?" Rena wanted to know.

"Seven guesses, sweetheart!" Gene laughed, putting his arm around her.

"Boy—and Ray said you were bashful!"

"Why, Ray—how could you?" Gene demanded, looking shocked; then he smiled. "It just goes to show you how wrong a person can be!"

They started up the steps that led to the second floor. In a few moments they were in their rooms.

"Well, Rena," Gene said, taking her in his arms, "How do you feel?"

"You should know that better than I do!" she cooed, pressing closer. "How *do* I feel?"

Her lips touched his and then parted.

The phone rang just then and Gene jerked in surprise. "Who can that be?"

"Shall we find out?" Rena asked brightly, moving to the bed. Taking the receiver, she said: "Hello?" A moment later Rena laughed. "The lodge wants to buy us a drink."

"Great!"

"What'll you have?"

"Scotch and soda."

"Scotch and soda—two of them," she ordered and hung up.

For a moment she sat on the edge of the bed and then suddenly she lay back, stretching her body full length on the double bed. "Oh boy—I'm tired."

She closed her eyes and then relaxed.

Gene looked down at the woman and felt a slight edge affection toward her. There was something about Rena that was very appealing. Beyond, of course, her lush figure. In fact he could see the nipples of her breasts pressing up tight against her sweater. There was more to the woman than mere, raw sexual energy—and a great body. Maybe it was because she was such a good sport—and fun. They'd had a ball coming up on the drive to the mountains. There had been singing and a bit of playful intimacy, with a kiss here and a soft, teasing caress there. Her hand had at one point boldly slipped between his thighs. "What's that?" she'd whispered in his ear. But nothing more. It was all playful tease, in a fun way. And it had been quite exciting.

Gazing down at her body, remembering how she had felt the night before, he wanted to fairly strip her naked and take her like a mad beast!

50

"What are you doing up there?" she asked, suddenly opening her eyes, and looking at him. "Why don't you come on down here?"

He didn't need a second invitation. His temples were throbbing.

Gene moved over to the bed and slid down next to her, slipping his arms around her body. She fairly ground up against him, sighing in pleasure of their lips met, tongues furiously seeking one another.

"Oh..." she fairly moaned in his ear a few moments later, lips touching the lobe. "I really want it...you!"

His hands stroked down her back, into the woman's buttocks, then back up her sides to her breasts.

"Yes..." was all she said, lips parted in anticipation of his kiss.

He sipped his hands up under her sweater and ran them along her naked breasts, since she'd not bothered to wear a bra. The feel of her flesh was soft, warm, supple under his fingers. She moaned, arched up against him, holding him tightly to her, then he felt the pressure of her fingers urging his head downwards in open invitation. She helped as he raised the sweater above her breasts, then grabbed his head, literally pushing him into them. A soft murmur of total pleasure uttered from her.

He thought he heard her sobbing, "Yes...oh.... Yes!" but it might have been his imagination, for his own mind was moaning such thoughts, wanting to simply drown in the sensation of this wildly passionate woman. Her own hands were frantically sliding down his back, then slipping between their bodies, searching eagerly for his belt. Then he felt her careless, or determined, fingers frantically search for the zipper, an act that rashly stroked the hardness under it. In fact she seemed to linger there with eager, bold intent, feeling the shape of him. She found and lowered the zipper and then her fingers slipped inside.

At that moment there was an annoying knock on the door.

"Christ!" Gene groaned as her hand move away from him.

"Probably the drinks!" She winked teasingly at where

her hand had been. "Best zip it!"

As he was doing just that, she quickly pulled her sweater back in place. "Better go get them."

He got up and opened the door.

"The drinks, sir," the bell-hop announced, stepping into the room.

Gene paid him a tip and quickly ushered the young man out of the room. Then he turned and walked over to the bed, handing one of the drinks to Rena.

"Well, here's to you!" he laughed, leaning over slightly and kissing her cheek. "I'd rather drink your…"

"Now, now. Be a gentleman!" she scolded.

"Are you kidding?" he boldly inquired, reaching out and cupping her breast through the sweater.

"Stop that!" she demanded, moving playfully away. "I want to drink right now."

She offered him a bright smile, then quickly pouted and added: "When I want you, I'll let you know!"

"Boy, you can sure be hard on a man!" he complained.

"I thought that's the man's job!

"What?"

"Being hard…well…on a woman, I suppose," she offered, all innocence.

He suddenly was confused. "What'd I say?"

"You said…I was hard on a man! Seems like it would be the other way around." She glanced down over his body, pointedly. "All things considered!"

They laughed and started drinking. He had to admit that Rena was a rather delightful lady, totally different from what he'd suspected when first considering her at the party the night before. It was totally impossible not to like her. Most confusing.

As the scotch settled in his stomach, Gene tried once more to figure out his feelings toward Rena. She was so different from the women he'd known in the past. They'd always been rather reserved and afraid. Maybe merely shy. She was neither reserved nor afraid. And certainly not in any way shy. Her brain worked on one type of fuel—that was sex. But with a delicious humor added to spice things up

52

quite a bit.

But was it only raw, naked passion, without any real deep emotion under-scoring it? Just the physical need of one animal for another? Was that all there could ever be between a man and Rena? That seemed so unjust. Strangely the more he got to know her the more dimensions he was noticing.

"What are you thinking about?" she asked, breaking his trend of thoughts.

"Oh—you. Of course. What else?"

"How nice!" she laughed. "But I don't believe you."

"*Really*, I was. Honest to God! Holy Truth. May the Force be with you. Hell, the force *is* with you!" He laughed at that. "And with a Wham Bam!"

"Hey, don't give me the old whamo bamboo, thank you mam-mo!" She laughed at that, then said: "Oh, sure! I'm Miss Wild Woman! Right?"

"You know, that's … well, what I thought. Well, not wild woman, just—"

"A bit loosie goosie?"

"Maybe, something like that, I suppose…" He sounded, even to himself, somewhat uncertain.

"And now?" she pushed, determined. "Now what do you think?"

He shrugged. "Getting to know you makes a dif?"

"Well don't get too tangled in all that. I am a wild woman at heart—and a real free spirited one, at that!" She considered him for a moment, and smiled. "You're okay, too. All things considered."

"Oh?"

"Well, Ray suggested you were all tied up in knots and needed some lady to loosen the…well…knots, so to speak!" She shrugged and that bounced her breasts under the sweater. She wiggled back and forth to make them really dance against the cloth, laughing at the expression on his face. "Like what you see, huh?"

"Can't help it. Can I?"

"You tell me. Tell me all. I love having a man devour me with his eyes." She threw back her head with a laugh, which thrust her breasts even tighter against the sweater.

She looked so delightful; so playful. She eyed him

with a warm smile, then took a sip of her drink.

He said: "You're quite a sport."

"Sport? Is that what you think of me? A sport?"

"I mean. Well, you're the first woman I've met who really knows how to make a man feel…well, really feel like a—man."

"In what way?" she asked, sitting up and moving her legs over the edge of the bed. She gazed up quite seriously at him.

"Oh, I don't know!"

"I think you do."

"Well, you are so different from the women I've known." He broke off too suddenly, looking away from her.

Silence followed, then: "So—it's another woman is it?"

He nodded, surprised she had so easily guessed what he had been about to say.

"Love her?"

"Love her—but never made the point!"

She nodded, knowingly. "I might have guessed."

She looked at him seriously for a second. "You're too nice a guy, Gene—you know."

"Sure—sure! Too nice a guy!" He looked down at his drink and then pulled it up to his lips and gulped it dry. "Let's not talk about it."

"Good idea!" she murmured in a low, soft voice, lying back on the bed. "I think maybe we better *really* change the subject!"

He looked at her for a long time before moving to the bed. Then found himself helplessly pulling her into his arms. He suddenly needed her to soothe away the ache. And it was actually Rena he needed and wanted. Nothing more.

She had some how removed her sweater and now playfully started to work on his pants, while laughingly saying: "I want what you're hiding down there!"

"I'm not…hiding," he chuckled as she started pulling zipper down.

"Well…I guess not!" she noted with a delightful glance into his eyes. "Not any more! What a delightful…prize you have for me."

54

He almost laughed at that, then felt a thrill rip up through his whole body. Her fingers took hold of what she'd just stripped naked.

"I love it!" she fairly moaned in delight. "Oh, how I love it. How I'll love it to death!"

"Geeze, Rena, not to death!" he managed, the words coming out so huskily that it was almost embarrassing. But not quite, for her hands were being warmly affection, tenderly showing how much she was enjoying him.

"Not...to...death, love." She murmured the words as her head moved towards her hands. "Just to its...total...limits. Oh, that's nice!"

Then as she breathed hotly against what her fingers so lovingly embraced. "Now..." she murmured, "your... mine..."

And suddenly she wasn't speaking. Her lips needed no words, for they were softly embracing him with eager caresses. After that the universe became nothing but a series of sensations, one after another. She was a lady determined to take her time, and she had the gentle and tense skill to know just how far to drive a man. Again and again he was pushed to the edge, only to have her back off just enough to tease him along another pathway to one wave after another of wonderful joyous pleasure.

He gasped as she lifted away and then straddled him. His eyes never opened once, for he was now swimming in a sea or unlimited joy. He never knew when her enveloped him deeply within her. Just, all at once, the hot warmth of the woman was drawing firmly around his whole being again and again, whipping electric fires around every nerve. It felt as if he were encased in some raging vice. And it would not let him go! And he *wanted* to be possessed by her.

He was aware of her movements, slowly building in their intensity, then backing off slightly, only to build again, more demandingly. Even when he felt the release buckle his body upwards, she continued without stop, not wanting to lose the prize she had so greedily owned. While the world, universe, seemed to explode over him, he was aware of the woman still embracing him, refusing to let go, thrashing now with very little control of her own. Then he became aware of once more growing tighter within her demanding flesh as it continued grinding hungrily around him.

She gasped, crying out in joy, lifting away to look down at him. The fiery glaze in her eyes was wild and savage as they feasted on what her flesh had recharged into full bloom.

"Oh, *honey*," she murmured, slowly laying on her back, in open offer. Her thighs parted, hips slightly squirming in anticipation, challenging him to take her.

Then he felt her legs lock about his hips, literally driving him deeply into her. His eyes closed against the thrilling pleasure.

He was totally beyond control. She cried out in the joyous ecstasy. No restraint was left between them. Now they were savages thrashing insanely at one another, powered by mindless need. At some point the two of them cried out, arching tightly together for one long, delicious moment. After that darkness ebbed and then he knew only that they were breathing as one, still locked in each another's arms, drifting deeper and deeper away from consciousness.

It would only be later, as he began to once again feel the world flow into being around him, that doubts surfaced. Slow, uncertain doubts about what had happened. Rena was overwhelming. Totally irresistible. Charming. Delicious. Hot. A fiery wanton. And such a skillfully caring lover. Demanding and amazingly caring about pleasuring her partner. And at the same time a complete blatant beast. She matched every moment, movement, breath, with a total awareness of how to take a man beyond all limits. He had never known a woman anywhere like her. And he doubted many men ever had the chance to experience such joyous pleasure. There weren't many women like this—most were either too shy or to self-centered to be so freely giving. At least that had been his experience, so far.

He had always heard that a woman should be a lady in the living room and a whore in bed. Rena was more than just that in bed. And something else in the "living room" as he'd discovered.

She was an ideal female to run to, to escape with, to totally satisfy the pain and need that could plague a man. She

56

was like a nurse to a wounded soul. The perfect mistress.

And he felt guilty about thinking of her in that way. At first he had believed it was necessary to be drunk take her to bed. The fact was that she could make a man drunk just taking her to bed.

He would want to have her again. That was without question. But it was basic, raw, selfish need.

He didn't want to admit to himself that he was running to her because he hadn't enough guts to force the issue with Pat. But one thing he knew, if he ever got the chance with Pat again he'd push things to the limit, and not leave them so totally unsatisfied.

Chances were, he realized, he'd probably never have another chance with Pat. For now it was Rena who could totally fill his needs.

What's more, he actually was beginning to like her, a lot.

He felt the woman move against him, and opened his eyes.

"Good morning," he offered, softly.

"Morning?"

"Well, okay, still light outside—but soon it'll be nightfall."

She murmured softly, then hugged to him. "Then we don't have to get out of bed, do we?"

He was stunned by the swift manner in which his body responded to her.

"Do we?" she giggled, letting her body communicate full awareness of his reaction to it. "My, is there no limit to you?"

He had to laugh at that. "That's your fault."

"Honey, babe, you'd be surprise." She hugged to him, kissed his cheek.

"How's that?"

"Not all men are so…well, you know what I mean!" Her hips pressed meaningfully to him. "See?"

"You're something," he said, desire raging through his nerves.

"I just love dat ol' six shooter you do have down there. Fully packed and ready to fire up again…and again. I mean, how many agains do ya have, pardner?"

"You an ol' cowhand, from the Rio Grande?" he laughed.

"No way, but I sure have a great firm fittin' holster fer dat fun gun ya have so boldly exposed...well...naughty boy!" she laughed, teasingly wiggling. "That's a pretty dangerous thing, ya know. Maybe we should take care of it. Want me to holster it for you?"

"Sure you can do that?"

"Are you kidding! I promise you. I can outshoot any gun-tottin' fella." Again she giggled with a little wiggle against him. She frowned, prettily. "Maybe not. All things considered."

"Like what?" he asked, letting his hand caress her breast.

"Well, darlin' ya sure do have some powerful weapon! Wildly impressive!"

They both laughed, then hugged one another in total delight. And completely aware of what was about to happen...again!

"Perhaps," she offered, with a pout, "we should hold off a little. Don't wanna unload the shooter too fast! We have a bit of time here in the mountains to enjoy one another....what do you think? Can you handle me again, or should be simply take a breather?"

"I thought you wanted to holster it."

"Well, I don't wanna wear it out too soon, ya know!"

At that point their lips met and they weren't about to continue that kind of conversation for a very long while.

XI.

THE RACE

Pat couldn't get over the beautiful setting slowly drifting below her as she sat in the chair of the ski-lift, being moved across the sky, far above the snowy hills, which were spotted with white-topped green trees. It was a sight that would always leave her slightly breathless; she would never get over her feeling of excitement of being up in the air, gliding toward a pinpoint high on a mountain top, held by a tiny moving wire. Even the prospect of skiing down the hills of white didn't really dull the thrill of watching, from this high vantage point in the sky, the many ant-like dots that were shooting down the mountainside on their way to the valley below. Soon she would be one of those little creatures, making her way in a never-ending twisting course, the wind blowing a youthful flush on her cheeks.

"Hi, there!" she heard Noel Anderson's voice call her from the chair in front.

She waved, smiling. Noel was nice, she thought. She couldn't help liking him—but that was really all she felt toward him. He was a nice guy who was taking her to a mountain cabin and then skiing, and, after that—who knew? Hopefully nothing she couldn't live with, later.

The way he had gotten her out of that jam the night before was nice, impressive. Most men wouldn't have bothered, especially after having turned him down for the date. Other men would have told her to jump in the lake. She wondered what Gene Bates might have done. It was silly the way he kept coming into her thoughts. She wanted to forget, and the more she tried, the worse it got. That might be the trouble—she was trying too hard.

The ski-lift suddenly loomed to a stop, sliding her toward the snowy surface of white. She stood and stepped out of the chair and walked over to where Noel was waiting.

"Well, quite a ride," she laughed, bending over and starting to put on her skis.

"Beautiful sites. I always love coming up here in the winter. There are so many things to do. Like at night you go on over to the lodge and have a large dinner drink, and then dancing. After that back to the cabin—"

"To town, you mean!" she quickly pointed out, only slightly alarmed.

His eyes dropped slightly as he said: "Sure—that's what I meant. Of course."

Somehow that sounded lame, but she determined to let it pass. Plus she felt sorta foolish having made such a statement. Yet as long as the man was controllable there certainly wasn't anything to be concerned about—except herself.

She shook that thought off, too. This wasn't why they had come up here to the top of the mountain, and she wasn't about to ruin the experience with mental fantasy issues that would probably prove groundless.

Pat stood straight and then announced, "All ready to fly!"

He stood up beside her and then the two of them started moving over to the edge of the sloping mountainside.

"I'll race you," Pat challenged, excitement toning her voice.

"How far?"

"All the way down to the lodge?"

"That's a deal!" he cried, smiling at her through the dark sunglasses over his eyes. "Bet you a cocktail that I beat you down!"

"Right!"

"Ready?"

"Ready!"

"One—two—three g-o-o-o-!" Noel shouted, starting

60

down the slope.

Pat gave him a slight lead and then started down the mountain, gaining speed with each flying second. It had been almost a year since she'd been skiing, and the last time had been with Gene.

Oh, dear, lovely, tame, gentleman Gene.

The wind brushed her cheeks, brightening them to a deep red glow. The frost was chilly in the air, but it made her feel wonderful and healthy. Skiing was one of the few sports that she went really wild about. That was one of the things that she and Gene had enjoyed so much. Why did she keep thinking about Gene? Maybe it was the snow. Maybe it was still too soon for her to forget.

Maybe…

But her thoughts shimmered as all attention focused on the downward journey into the valley below.

Her eyes focused consciously on the speeding snow and the passing trees. She glided in and out, weaving between trees and other skiers.

Pat looked for a sign of Noel, but he had disappeared. There were many ways down the mountain to the lodge, and she and Noel each must have taken a different one.

The excitement of the race now pushed out the thoughts of Gene and her still strongly confused emotions about the man. Only one thought raced through her now:

Win!

Not that it mattered, but it was a point of pride. If she could win...

She would!

But why was it a point of pride? She pushed that thought from her mind. She didn't like the word pride. She never had. Her mind focused once more on the snow-covered mountain below her. It would be a long trip down; a long, beautiful trip of being alone with her own thoughts. Challenged by the mountain and the snow.

She suddenly flew over a slight rise and shot into empty air. A stab of excitement shot through her as she landed back on the snow. Expertly, she remained standing, still rushing downwards toward her meeting with destiny...

Any <u>One</u> Can Die! by Charles Nuetzel

XII.

THE MEETING

Gene was sitting at the bar next to Rena, when Ray and June came down from their room to join them. All were dressed now in ski clothes. It was still early in the afternoon.

"Well, hello there, Ray, my buddy!" Gene cried.

"What are you two drinking?"

"Martinis. What are you having?"

"Same, I believe!" Ray looked at June, questioningly. The girl just nodded her sexy little dark head.

Gene called the bartender and ordered. "I understand," he said a moment later, "that they don't like people going up too late after dark—unless they're good skiers."

"Except for Balding Mountain. They had a range lighted there," Ray told him.

"That's for chickens. If it's moonlight tonight a guy can see well enough—"

"No skiing tonight," the bartender's voice told them, breaking into the conversation as he laid down the four martinis.

"What the—How's that?" Gene wanted to know.

"Snowing. The weather man says something about a storm. A heavy storm. It's supposed to break before it turns dark. If that happens then there'll be no skiing for anybody! So if you're going to do it, best to do it fast!"

Gene looked at Rena and then at Ray. "That does it for our moonlight ride!"

"Hell, don't let that bother you—there are other

63

things to do around here!" Ray laughed, indicating Rena.

The woman smiled, knowingly, as his eyes met hers. The second time around had left both of them fully sated— for the moment.

"I take it you two were swingin' wildly. You aren't tired of one another...yet?

"Hardly," Rena announced, patting Gene's arm. "He's a mighty warrior and I am doing my best of counter every one of his...well, you know how it is with great swordsmen!

"Yeah, yeah," Ray offered, "just one thrust after another!"

"My," Rena said in a shocked voice: "Were you peeking? Shame on you!"

They all laughed at that.

"I was doing a bit of fencing with this nice lady!" Ray said. "No time to look in on your match and mate bout! But I'm not against tryin' ya out just for the hell of it!"

Gene didn't like Ray's comment. It made her appear trampish. Sure, she was a wild free sprit, but hardly a tramp! He felt annoyed at the automatic defensive reaction to Ray's words. He wanted to bash the man in the face.

Silly, that, Gene admitted to himself. *Give the guy a break.*

"Anybody hungry?" he asked, trying to change the subject.

"Why not since night skiing is out!" Ray offered. "Replenish the ol' bod for the ... games to follow!"

"Not a bad idea!" Rena echoed, raising her glass to her lips. Then she ran a finger along his cheek, while watching Ray's reaction. "I can't wait. And I can't thank you enough for the intro! He's a real class-A Zeppo!"

Ray laughed at that. "Zeppo Marks?"

"Well, not that funny, but just as much fun, if not more so. Actually," she continued, "I never knew any of the Marks Brothers in that way. You know, intimately or anything like that. They were way past my bedtime."

June piped in: "Bedtime? What did they...?"

"Old movies. Don't you remember them?" Rena challenged. "Late TV. A lot of slap stick and satire. Groucho

64

was a wild one."

"And," Ray noted, "Chico was supposed to be quite a hot lady's man!"

"I think they all were," Rena offered. "In their day they must have really enjoyed quite a wild life."

"But," Ray offered, patting June's thigh, "not any more wild than we can enjoy."

Rena shrugged that off, offering: "I enjoyed those old films, though. And they were quite a laugh. But the only slap stick I need is the one right here next to me! Still, I really enjoyed those old films. I'm a kinda fan of them, even if they were a bit…silly and some what prudish—I mean, of course, those old ones back in the black and white days! Before the R- and X-rated ones we can rent on DVDs. "

June shrugged it off with: "Oh. X or not, I'm not too much into that. Just into…well, real, live men, I suppose."

"And I'm not? Honey you sure don't know me!"

Ray said: "Right, June, she's been…"

"Never you mind," Rena scolded, waving a finger in the air. "I can advertise my own rep—without any help from the audience, thank you!"

They all kinda forced a light laugh.

Rena shrugged it all off with a light smile, glanced at Ray and said: "So, let's go skiing!"

"Remember? It's out tonight!" Ray reminded her.

"I mean, now. Just a little. It'll be a while before it gets dark. And the sky looks pretty clear, still," she noted, looking out the huge windows which made up one wall of the lodge, revealing the mountainside.

They all considered that, realizing there might be time to enjoy a quick afternoon ski.

"Okay then—to skiing!" Gene toasted, taking a large swallow of the cocktail.

"Do you really think it's safe?" June asked, worried sounding. "I'm not really much of a skier, you know. Just a beginner."

"Oh, don't be silly, my dear, I've seen you! Great. You'll do!" Ray laughed, placing an arm around her shoulder and pulling her closer. "We won't go up too high, and I'll keep right behind you so that if anything happens you'll be safe. Keeping my eye on your lush behind will make—"

"You blind!" June laughed back. 'Thanks—just let's not have anything bad happen."

The four downed their drinks and then started to turn to leave.

That's when Gene felt as if a hammer had been rammed into his gut.

He went suddenly stiff, shock showing on every feature of his face.

Pat Taylor and Noel Anderson had just stepped into the cocktail lounge, arm in arm, laughing like two happy children.

XIII.

KILL NUMBER TWO

As Helen pointed the gun in the direction of the doctor, his face turned grim. "This won't get you anyplace, young lady."

"I'm just not taking any chances," she told the man, motioning him to freeze. "If you try to walk out on us again, I might have to use this."

She'd been at the doctor's home for a couple of hours. It was the first place she had come across since Carl had been injured by the near car accident. He was still unconscious; but alive. That was one thing to be thankful for. She'd finally found it necessary to stop at a gas station and get the directions to the nearest doctor's home.

It had been only a matter of moments to get Carl into the house, with the doctor's help. Everything was running along smoothly, the doctor accepting her lies about what had happened—when Carl started mumbling under his breath.

"I think he's coming out of it," the doctor had told her.

The words were hard to understand at first, and then Carl raised up slightly, dazed, looking blankly into the room. "The money...the bank money!" he cried. "Don't forget the money!"

"What's he talking about?" the doctor asked, turning to Helen.

She tried to look innocent and confused. And then Carl really blew the lid off things by saying: "After all the work with the holdup—don't forget the money!"

Then he dropped downwards on the bed where the doctor had placed him.

The medical man looked at Helen. "So you're the ones. I heard something about the hold-up this morning."

"So—what are you going to do about it?" she demanded, nastily.

That's when he went to the phone. Crossed the front room and reached for the phone.

She'd pulled out the gun and ordered: "Don't be foolish. I'll use it. A promise!"

She didn't know what she would do with him; that would be Carl's problem when he came back to consciousness.

A shiver moved through her at the thought of what might happen. What Carl might have to do the man. She didn't like killings; she wanted nothing to do with them. But there might be nothing she could do about this doctor's plight. If it was his life or theirs, she didn't doubt her own ability to pump him full of bullets.

It was several hours before Carl Anderson moved again. This time his eyes opened wide—jerking in their swift search of the room.

"What happened?" he demanded, trying to sit up.

The doctor leaned over and said kindly enough, "You've had a bad bump on the head. You'll be okay, if you take care of yourself."

Carl looked at the doctor, a frown creasing his forehead.

"Who's he?"

"A doc," Helen told him.

Carl looked in the direction of the woman and then saw the gun in her hands, pointed at the other man.

"What's that for?" was his only question.

"You got to talking—and the doctor heard. He was going to call the police!"

Carl looked at the man again, his eyes squinting. "That's too bad, Doc. Really too bad. A real shame, that is."

He started to rise.

"Take it easy, son," the doctor told him, trying to

hold him back.

"Keep your goddamn hands off me!" Carl cried, brushing the other man away from him. "And don't tell me what to do!"

He stood, weaving drunkenly. "Can you give me something for a headache?"

"Of course—if you don't mind my giving it to you." There was a slight edge of sarcasm in the doctor's voice.

"Chop it, doctor-man! Just get the pills and be damned quick about it!"

The doctor turned and started for the bathroom just off the room they were in.

"And don't try anything!" Carl told him, motioning to Helen to give him the gun.

A second later the doctor returned, handed Carl the pills and then stepped carefully backwards as he saw the gun in his hand.

"It's too bad, doc, that you had to hear too much!" Carl told him. "Give me the silencer!" he demanded of Helen.

A gasp sounded from her. "It's in the car—our car...I had to leave it back on the road."

Carl turned frantically to her. "What do you mean? You forgot the money, too?"

Just then he felt the impact of a man's fist slice across his jaw. For a moment the world spun horribly before his eyes and then without thinking he pulled the trigger of his gun that was pointed directly at the dark blotch which was the doctor. The bullet went into the man's stomach and he shot backwards, hitting the table behind him.

Carl's vision cleared and he looked at the dying doctor.

"Too bad, Doc!" he cursed, kicking out at the man's face. His foot caught at the nose, ripping it wide from the rest of the man's features. "Docs that know too much get themselves killed!"

He aimed the gun at the doctor's bloody face and pulled the trigger. The features exploded red and then the head went limp.

"Let's get the hell out of here!" he cried, turning to

Helen who was leaning on the edge of the bed, her face white with terror and shock, her hand over her mouth

"Come on you bitch!" he cursed, moving to her and taking hold of her shoulder. Roughly he shoved her forward. She resisted weakly and without warning he turned on her, slapping her across the face with the back of his hand which held the gun. "Come on—we don't have time!"

She whimpered as blood trickled out of her mouth. An evil, hateful expression twisted her eyes to insane ugliness.

But she followed him without a word or struggle.

ACT FOUR

ANY ONE CAN DIE! BY CHARLES NUETZEL

XIV.

INTERPLAY

Pat felt as if she'd been slapped by a chilly wind as they stepped into the lodge. She went icy cold inside.

All thoughts of the race, and the fact that she had gotten to the lodge just a few moments before Noel, froze in her mind. She couldn't believe what she was seeing.

Gene Bates was standing at the bar with three other people. The woman who stood next to him was a real comer, even if a bit on the cheap side. She probably slept with any man who fancied her. And men would go for her type!

That really hurt.

She couldn't help feeling a stab of jealousy, even though she realized that Gene had just as much right to be out with a woman as she had to be out with Noel—or any man, for that matter.

Still it hurt her pride to find out that he was so obviously enjoying himself—as if it didn't really matter to him that they had broken up.

Especially after she had been thinking so much about him.

Her first reaction was to freeze, outwardly as well as inwardly. Then suddenly she smiled, forcing the reaction of her facial muscles to bring the corners of her lips upwards.

"Why, look who's here!" she exclaimed in a bright voice that she hoped sounded light and airy. The last thing she wanted Gene to know was that she felt so hurt.

Taking hold of Noel's arm she dragged him after her,

stepping right up to Gene and his friends. "Why, how nice to see you. What a lovely surprise!"

The expression on Gene's face was blank as he looked at her. Then finally he smiled, and she couldn't help thinking that it seemed a little forced. Actually very forced!

And no wonder, she thought, *caught in the act!*

"Why, hello, Pat," he said stiffly. "How'd you happen to be here?"

It sounded more like he was accusing her of following him, rather than the fact that this was a complete accident.

"It's a free world! And, anyway, you know I like skiing!" she snapped back, showing anger in the bitter edge of her tone of voice.

"That's what we came up here for," he stated, lamely.

The woman next to him smiled quite warmly, as she looked from one to the other. "Gene's a ball. Just love the man!"

"I'm glad you're enjoying him!" Pat snapped back, not even looking at the woman. Her eyes were searching Gene's, trying to find some pain, some hurt, some feeling. Nothing showed. "He's such a nice guy. But..." and now she glanced at the woman, "I'm surprised he's *your* type of man."

"Oh? What do you think is my type?" the woman inquired, taking Gene's arm, hugging it close to her.

Pat shrugged, as if it didn't matter and didn't require a verbal retort.

"He suits me just fine. Don't you, honey?"

"Sure thing," Gene managed in a forced, but agreeable voice. "We get alone, just fine."

Noel broke in for the first time. "If you don't mind, dear—I don't believe I know these people."

For the next few moments introductions were quickly made all around and Pat realized what a mistake she had made by not ignoring Gene. It looked like they were going to be together for a while, and it was the last thing that she wanted—being even near Gene. At this time it was the worst thing that could have ever taken place. She wanted to forget Gene; that's why she'd come up to the mountains with Noel.

74

It wasn't fair! But she wasn't about to show her confusion—or her dislike of what was taking place. The best thing she could do was act like everything was fine.

"Say," Noel said, "Why don't you all come to my place for a party tonight, that is, if you're planning to stay that long."

"We have rooms, but—" Gene started to say.

Pat quickly spoke, before she really had a chance to think things out. "Sure—why don't you. It would be great fun!"

The sound of her voice had an edge of challenge to it, and from the expression on Gene's face she was sure that he caught it. For the first time she guessed at his emotional reaction to the situation. Now she wished she had nixed the idea, right off. But it was too late for that.

"Okay!" Gene announced hurriedly, as if wanting to show her that she couldn't out-bluff him. "How about it, Rena, darling?"

Rena gave him a large smile and nodded her head eagerly. "As long as we're together...I'm for it!"

Ray looked at June and then at Gene. "Okay—why not?"

Gene asked: "But first—what about the skiing?"

"It's pretty windy out, Mr. Bates," Noel told him.

"Call me Gene—"

"First names all around?" Noel suggested. And that closed the issue.

"Skiing out?" Rena asked, hardly disappointed.

"It might be a good idea—with the storm coming?" Ray put in, pulling June closer. "And anyway, I'm hungry."

"Have you two eaten?" Gene asked, looking directly into Pat's eyes.

She felt an inner quiver shake through her, but held down any physical sign of it. She didn't want to expose the hurt that she was feeling seeing Gene with such a sexy blonde. And so obviously enjoying the woman's company. The way Rena hugged to him made it quite obvious that she considered him totally hers. At least for the night. Finally Pat realized that everybody was waiting for her answer to Gene's question.

"What do you think?" she asked Noel.

"I'm a bit hungry—skiing builds up a good appetite!"

Gene exploded in an overly anxious voice: "*Great!* Why not go into the dining room now!"

Everybody took up the suggestion and a few moments later they were sitting at a large table, appearing on the surface like old friends who hadn't seen each other for years. Yet Pat felt the undercurrent of emotional strain. Maybe it was her imagination, but it seemed as though Gene kept giving her side-long glances throughout the meal—but she wasn't sure because she didn't really dare look his way unless it was completely necessary. And she made sure that didn't happen very often.

* * * * * *

Gene's first reaction to seeing Pat had been stunned surprise; and then a second feeling came over him—a feeling of total nausea; she was the last person he wanted to see— anybody but Pat Taylor, the woman he was trying so hard to forget. He found himself not only roped into a dinner but an evening at Noel Anderson's cabin. And so he started ordering extra martinis.

"Haven't you had enough?" Rena hissed softly, kicking him in the leg under the table.

Wasn't that just like a woman—the minute you become nice to them, they want to take over; they didn't know the fine line between being nice and being interested, he thought. Still he played it for all it was worth.

"Why, honey," he said in a loud voice, "let's make with the happy times—it is seldom that a man gets a chance to be with an attractive woman up in the mountains, a storm on the edge of breaking around us. Just think of the excitement! All trapped together! How..."

"Intimate?" Pat offered, rather blandly.

"Yes...I suppose so," was his lame retort.

Rena giggled with delight. "Very, very intimate, if you ask me. Of course, you didn't ask, but who cares. I love the mountains and the snow and the idea of being together with...friends, even if they're all new friends...well what

76

could be better? Huh, Gene?"

That last she accented under the table with her hand caressing along his thigh.

"Sure, yes, yes," he said, wanting to push her hand away. He wanted to scream, not right now. Yet another side of him was kind of pleased that Rena was playing it close to the chest, so to speak. He guessed she knew what was between him and Pat. Her fingers caressed him lightly, then patted him rather tenderly, in a friendly manner.

He glanced at her and as their eyes connected she seemed to silently indicate a quite understanding.

"Gene," she offered, "I think you're wonderful. Really, I do!"

Rena didn't move her level gaze from him, but there was every reason to believe the words were really directed at Pat, sitting just to his right.

Ray suddenly blurted: "Well, I don't know about the rest of you, but I'm all for a party! Best we gather together the troops before the blizzard lands in our laps!"

Noel looked at his watch and then said, "That's a point. We should get on over to my place—before it does break. It is getting late and I understand that the storm is due to hit here early this evening. It was starting up at the top— or rather halfway, when we were skiing."

Everybody took up the suggestion and the bill was paid. After Noel had given directions to his place, he and Pat left. Gene's group was to follow in their own car in a few minutes—and the delay suited Gene fine. He wanted to get a little more plastered before he had to face Pat again.

"Let's buzz up to the hotel room and dig into our liquor supply," he suggested to the others.

"Grand idea. I could use another," Ray exclaimed, taking June's arm and falling in behind Gene and Rena.

Gene kept his attention on Rena's lush body; it was his only defense against Pat. If he could keep focused on her, that would help one hell of a lot.

When they were in their room, Gene pulled out a small case and opened it.

"Say," he said in as casual a voice as possible, "Why don't you girls change into something real wild. Something neat. I'd like people to see the kind of women I go around with!"

There was a nervous laugh behind him. He turned. It was Rena. "What are you laughing at?"

"You, dear Gene!"

"Why?" Anger raced up his face.

"It's quite obvious that you still madly in love with her!"

"Who?"

"Pat—whatever her name was!"

Ray cut in with: "Lay off, Rena! Give the guy a break!"

"Oh, what difference does it make? We all aren't kids. Gene and I are great fun together; nothing more. Well, okay, super fun! But I'm not the jealous type." She turned to Gene, added: "You should know that by now, honey. I think it's just one hell of a laugh, though."

Ray stepped up to Rena. "I said to lay off! Maybe it's the best thing that happened to Gene. Maybe he needs a chance to face the fact that he and Pat run around with other people. That he doesn't need Pat and Pat doesn't need him. Maybe he'll get the idea that she's not the kind of woman he thought she was!"

Gene just stood there looking at the other three. Shock showed on his face. "I don't get it. What are you guys trying to do?"

"Help you out a little—that's all!" Ray said.

"How?"

"Just have a good time!" Ray turned to Rena. "I asked you to help him out—and..."

"What the hell!" Gene snapped. "Ray!"

"Hey, don't take it out on me!" Ray explained, looking back to Gene. "I just wanted to help—"

"Stop helping!" Gene snapped. "I'm a big boy!"

"Yeah, you said it. Boy in a man's body!" Ray almost growled the words. "Oh, hell, sorry, man."

Rena offered: "You should be. He's a great man, if you ask me!"

"Well, then..." Ray shrugged. "What's the issue? You two...seem to be getting along just grand!"

78

To Gene, Rena said, quite seriously: "He just said that you'd broken up with a doll and needed a woman to help bring you out of it. I kinda told you all that, last night! Or was it this afternoon. I forget. You're been ringing me like wild, honey. Enjoy. Ray's right about that. Have fun." Rena explained in a softer voice.

Gene looked down, then back up at her. "I guess so. Sorry you two."

June exploded happily: "Well about time! You had me frightened."

"Why so?" Ray wanted to know.

"Well, party time and you're clawing at one another like a bunch of rabid gorillas!"

They laughed at that, relieved at the change of subject.

Rena's face brightened. "Okay, lover, I'll dress the sexiest you've ever seen me. Well, in clothing, that is! I'll keep your mind off that little iceberg!" She laughed. "I really don't see what you saw in her. I bet she has a real hot kiss! A steaming goodnight peck!"

Gene laughed, because it was pretty much the truth— or at least for the first three or four kisses it had been.

He laughed, too, because he was suddenly nervous and needed some outlet.

But he felt a harsh inner pain at laughing at Pat. Still he shook it off by reasoning that she really deserved it.

A little prude that wouldn't put out for the man she loved because she was afraid. Of what?

And that was a laugh!

What was she afraid of? he argued with himself, determined to somehow get through the evening with some class.

He glanced at Rena, who smiled knowingly, as if reading his mind. She nodded, shrugged to let her breasts wiggle, and promised: "We'll have a good time, no matter what!"

"Okay," Gene offered, forcing himself to relax. Maybe things would work out. "Make me proud of you!"

"I promise!" she assured him. "And you know I can do wonders with a man!"

She came close, let her lips brush his. "I really like being with you, Gene. Honest!"

He gazed warmly into her eyes, feeling real tenderness and something more, which was hard to define, other than he really liked her, too. She was making no demands on him, other than enjoying what she had to offer. And it was a lot, even more than one hell of a sexy lady. For somebody he had just met, he felt as if she were a real friend.

And a man wanted a woman who knew how to use her body; a woman who enjoyed sex and all the things which involved sex. Love; romance; and getting into bed and acting like—like Rena!

That was the type of wife Gene wanted and that was the reason that he and Pat had broken up. Sure, she had been the one who had done the walking, but maybe she had been right.

"Snap out of it, Gene," Ray told him, slapping him on the shoulder.

He focused on Ray's boyish features. Then he looked around. "Where are the girls?"

"Went to my rooms; changing there. We can drink ourselves into a slight case of drunkenness."

"That suits me just fine!" Gene exploded, starting to fix drinks and not allowing himself to think about the fact that he must have been standing like a stone statue for a very long time—not even realizing that the girls had left Ray and himself alone.

He needed a drink! That's what he needed. A good strong drink.

"Say, Ray—I've been thinking about that job offer you had. You know—in your dad's insurance company— San Fran?"

"Okay, Gene. Anytime you want. But believe me, you'll just be running away from her."

"I know," he admitted, a but confused. "I should have followed her and tried to get her back."

"Too late for that! She's taken!" Ray pointed out. "Noel seems like a nice sort."

"I suppose," was all Gene could say to that.

Ray said: "Look, leaving town won't help. Learn to

deal. This accidental meeting is the best thing that could have happened to either of you!"

Gene nodded, refilling his drink.

"Sure, sure," he said bitterly. "Sure—the best thing that could have ever happened!"

Any One Can Die! by Charles Nuetzel

XV.

KICKS, BABY, KICKS

Carl Anderson and Helen had managed to escape into their car without anybody really noticing them soon enough to be any threat. The gun shots had attracted attention, but as it is so many times true, most people thought at first it was only a car backfiring. By the time anybody really figured out what had happened, Carl had already put a long distance between himself and the doctor's house.

Helen sat in the seat next to him, blank and white faced.

"You didn't have to kill him!" she moaned.

"What's with you, babe? I thought you knew the score. If the police get me—I'm baked. I'll burn like hell."

"But why...why did you have...have to kill him the way you did?"

"Kicks, baby. Kicks!" After a moment he added: "So shut up about it."

There was a long silence. Neither spoke. Then finally Carl pulled the car to a sudden stop and got out. He moved around to Helen's side.

"You'll have....have to drive, baby. My head hurts like hell. Those damned pills that bastard gave me didn't do no good."

She slid over and put the car into gear.

"You'll live," she announced coldly.

"What kind of a remark is that?" he growled, looking hard at her.

"You aren't dead. That's all!" she explained, a light bitterness edging her voice. "So stop complaining!"

"You're damned right I'm not dead. And I don't intend to be dead. Nobody—but nobody will stop me...I'd kill my own brother—even you, if you got in my way! But of course, I'm not worried about that. You're my baby!"

"How much farther to the cabin?" she asked, directing the car up to the mountain turn-off.

"Twenty—thirty minutes. Depends."

A mist clouded the windshield and Helen turned on the wipers. "Bad weather."

"It'll be hell! Snowed in—real deep! That'll make things a bit easier. One hell of a lot easier. Let the cops look all over the country for us and we'll be having a ball, boozing it up in a snowed-in cabin. I can't wait to get myself all lost in your hot body!"

He pawed her thigh, possessively. "We'll be safe there, alone together for the duration! All snowed in and comfortable. Plenty of time to really enjoy one another to the fullest."

"How come you're so sure about the snow?"

"Weather report. I checked on it." He paused for a moment and then laughed. "You aren't the only one with brains, baby. Not the only one!"

"Sure. Sure."

XVI.

THE GAMES BEGIN

Pat tried to laugh, be lighthearted as she dressed. But thoughts of Gene kept ripping apart the gay mood that had been so wonderful a few hours before the accidental meeting.

With conscious care she picked her most sensually revealing dress.

She'd teach Gene, her mind promised. *Then he'd know what kind of woman he was missing!*

Pat was almost finished when Noel Anderson's voice sounded from behind the door: "Ready?"

"Almost!" Pat called back.

She quickly made up her face, arranged the top of the dress so it was more revealing about her breasts and then stepped out into the front room of the cabin.

"I'll take a drink, now, Noel!" she announced, suddenly aware of how greatly she needed one.

"Sure!" Before he turned to fix the drinks he added: "You look fantastic. Simply great!"

After fixing drinks, Noel stood before the roaring fire he had started when they returned to the cabin.

"Wonder what's keeping your friends," he commented, after taking a swallow of the highball in his hands.

"I'm glad they're taking their time."

Noel frowned. "What's with you and...this Gene fellow?"

"What in the world makes you ask that?" she de-

85

manded defensively, trying to avoid explanations.

"Everybody noticed. You were quite nasty—"

"It's none of your business!"

His eyes frowned but a light laugh broke from his mouth. "Hit pay dirt did I? Thought so."

'Please, oh please drop the subject," Pat managed in a small voice.

"Sure, sure," he quickly promised, half raising his hands in a shrug. "There's no reason for us to ruin a fun vacation over...well—"

"The past! Nothing more! So let's forget it!" she offered in a bright voice—much too bright.

In an effort to clear the air, Pat moved over to the fire, standing next to Noel. He looked at her for a long moment, then said in a warm voice, "You're quite a lovely woman. I never guessed how attractive you really are."

He leaned toward her, his arms slid around her body, and he started to pull her impulsively closer. Then his lips moved toward hers. At that point she decided to submit to him. That was the best way to satisfy the man that Gene meant nothing to her. She parted her lips to his.

Just then there was a loud banging on the front door.

"Damn!" was Noel's only word as he moved away. A moment later he opened the door and let in his guests. Then as he turned to close the door a gust of wind blew inwards, keeping the door open. "Give me a hand—somebody!"

The two other men helped Noel and after a few seconds struggle they managed to close the door and latch it.

"I'll tell you," Ray exploded, quickly moving over to the fire and rubbing his hands together, "it is chilly and windy and one hell of a storm starting outside!"

Pat didn't pay much attention because her eyes were locked with Gene's for a moment. The two of them just stood, silently looking at each other. Then Rena tugged on Gene's arm, smiling and playfully kissing him on the cheek. "Come on—it's a lot warmer over here!"

The implication of that remark didn't miss Pat. She smiled nicely and sweetly said: 'Why, Rena, dear—how in the world would you know?"

"That's not so hard—just look at the poor boy...all

86

chilled and cold. He needs a little warm up—and I'm the girl who knows how to!"

And that ended that—for the moment, anyway.

"Well, how about drinks for everybody?" Noel suggested in a loud voice, while rubbing his hands together. "Highballs for you folks?"

Gene nodded and then the other three followed his example. There was a silence while Noel fixed the drinks and then he handed the tall glasses around and went over to the stereo in the corner of the room. In seconds the soft sounds of music filled the air.

"Whatever you want to do—dance—booze...help yourselves!—or just talk! Anyway—do what you want!" Noel turned down the lights so that most of the dim glow came from the warm fireplace. "Now—how's that?"

"Great!" Ray exclaimed, taking June in his arms and giving her a light kiss on the lips; then he pulled her away from the fire and started to slowly dance.

Noel quickly took up the example by stepping to Pat's side. She was more than willing to have something to do other than just stand there trying desperately to keep from looking in Gene's direction. The heat and anger raging from her verbal exchange with Rena was still painful.

She didn't notice when Gene started dancing, but suddenly he was moving in gentle rhythm with the music, Rena was clinging flush up against him. The woman was moving her hips, almost in a rubbing fashion, against Gene's. Her lips were nibbling on his earlobe.

"What's the matter, Pat?" Noel whispered in her ear. "You're all tense. Relax!"

"Sorry," she whispered, forcing herself to move closer to him, trying to relax in his arms.

Noel seemed to rock harder against her, his thigh moving in against hers. Then his lips caressed her neck and she couldn't help feeling a mild shiver of excitement burn through her. His lips felt soft and warm. But she held down the urge to surge against him in response; she didn't want to start something that she might have to stop.

Then her eyes caught Gene's and the look on his face caused her to boldly surge closer to Noel.

Gene's face seemed to be a shade of green in the dim light.

He was jealous as hell! she realized, delighted. *Oh, God, he's so jealous!*

And just seeing the look he was giving her was enough to cause a thrill to shoot through every nerve.

Or was she reacting to Noel's hard form?

It really didn't make any difference. She felt light headed, and that was enough.

She knew it was necessary to play up to Noel like hell. That would show Mister Gene Bates that he wasn't the only man in the world.

Stop it, Pat! she screamed at herself, forcing all attention to return to Noel. She pressed herself tighter to him and he responded by gently kissing her neck.

This was going to be one hell of a night. That much she knew. A long evening of trying to play games so that Gene Bates would never know how much she really cared. How much she hurt. Wanted him.

Pat did everything she could to keep her eyes away from Gene's.

She had to keep from looking at him. She just had to!

Pat melted against Noel, and their bodies seemed to fuse deliciously. She was surprised at how nice he actually did feel. That was unexpected. She looked up at the man, wondering. Was she that fickle?

No, Pat told herself. *Just human.*

She hurt so much that the feel of any man so closely held, so intimately responding to her in such a blatantly obviously way, was suddenly very appealing.

Better than being painfully alone, she tried to convince herself.

But the way things were going, it wouldn't be long before she'd have to decide just how far this game must be played. It was, in its way, rather fun to be flirtatious in such an open manner.

The feel of him against her was almost embarrassing. Men would be shocked about how easily they exposed their animal needs. They were so obvious it was funny.

Noel whispered in her ear, "Easy, Pat, a man can take

so much."

Innocently, she blurted, a bit too loud, "Take what?"

Then she turned pink, all over. Embarrassed.

He had pressed closer to her, this time an obvious action to let her know exactly what he meant. She was painfully aware of his hard muscular body. He didn't have to say "feel that!"

She wanted to scream, *Please don't!*

But instead she merely let her arms slip around his waste, though she didn't press closer. Some how the message seemed to connect with the man.

"You okay?" he asked.

She felt weak inside, wanting comfort, not brazen sexual contact. But how could she communicate that to him? Instead she said nothing, now merely held close to the man, more to hide the tears threatening to burst from her eyes.

The music suddenly came to a climax and ended.

She instantly slipped away from Noel, relieved the dancing was over for now. She turned, looking at the fire. A mistake, cause the man's arms circled her body, drawing her back against him. She felt him so powerfully that it was almost scary. She didn't dare move a muscle for fear of doing something that might communicate the wrong message. How could she get away from him?

"Noel," she murmured, softly, "I could use a drink."

"Sure. Sorry. I'm being a terrible host!" He moved away, but took her hand warmly in his, drawing her after him. "Come, we'll fix something for you."

"Thanks," was all she said, following him.

Somehow a message seemed to have connected with the man. He said: "Easy, Pat. Nobody is pushing anything…I just want to work things out nice with you."

"Thanks, again," she offered softly. "It isn't you."

"I know, darn it!" He chuckled. "But hell, what can I expect? We just connected. Let's be friends, at least."

"Of course. Boss." She smiled, as he slipped behind the bar, holding her total attention to him.

"Boss?" he shuttered visibly, laughing, and said: "I hardly want to you think of me only in that way. You're a free agent. We're just two people—work isn't until…that's right, I'd forgotten. Tuesday. Monday is a holiday."

He turned to the others, who had come up to join them. "Hey we have a couple of days, here, now. Guess we'll all become pretty friendly before the weekend if over."

With the skill of a trained bartender, Noel delivered glasses to each of them, nicely filled with whiskey and soda. "Well, salute to a lovely bunch of coconuts! Down the hatch and let's celebrate our mutual isolation in this quiet little cabin of mine!"

The man had his eyes locked with Pat's as he said the last. "Time to enjoy life! Don't you think?"

They all lifted their drinks in mutual salute as the crash of thunder sounded from outside.

"Best enjoy while we can!" Ray noted.

Rena laughed: "We'll all have to hug close together to keep warm, I suppose."

Pat took a gulp on the drink, said: "Hopefully not too close!"

The other woman laughed that off, said: "Honey, nothing like a hot bod to keep a girl from freezing! And I don't expect to freeze this night away!"

Pat glanced at Rena as she hugged close to Gene like a woman taking possession of her personal property. She was saying in no uncertain terms: *this is my man!*

Hiding her own fury, Pat looked at Noel, who was standing just in front of her, only the counter between them. Maybe that made her feel safe and secure. She blurted: "Well, I got me my body warmer!"

"Me too!" June exploded, gripping Ray's arm. "Me too!"

90

XVII.

BROTHERS MEET

Carl Anderson still felt the throbbing ache in the front of his head where the skin was tight with a hard bruised lump, but the pills were finally beginning to dull the pain a little. He looked out at the snowy road.

"Don't this thing have chains?" he cursed.

"I didn't think about such things," Helen told him. "All I could think of was getting somebody to help you...I almost forgot the money."

"Great. Just great!" He thought for a moment. "It's not too far to the cabin. Just about a mile now. Take it easy. Slow and easy," he directed her. "Maybe we can make it through the snow without any trouble. It's not too thick right now. But it will be—it will be!" he laughed, patting her thigh. "Baby, we're gonna have one wild time!"

* * * * * * *

Gene Bates was fairly high, and the shock of seeing Pat so beautifully dressed, so sensually presented in the silky red sheath was more than he could stand. He hadn't expected her to be so boldly displayed; it didn't seem like the Pat Taylor he thought he'd known.

The emotions were much too great for his half drunk mind to be able to handle, and for the first time he was more than thankful to Rena for being there with him.

One thing he realized: Pat and he were playing a hor-

91

ridly brutal game with each other, and he was determined to keep from letting her bother him, at least outwardly. He didn't dare let her know the truth; to let her win would be too much of a loss. Still it was hard not to look her way; drink in the total beauty of this lady he wanted too badly and now had lost! And it was even harder to see her so damned affectionate with Noel.

For the first time in his life he could see how easily he could learn to hate another person, even if Noel was actually quite a nice guy. It certainly wasn't that man's fault for going for Pat.

Somehow he managed to keep from getting too plastered. He wanted to let his mind get lost in the raw, erotic pleasure of Rena's body. That was his only weapon, he reasoned, his only way of keeping emotional sanity.

Now he realized much he needed Pat; life without her was empty. Those feelings hadn't been false; but very real. Only there seemed no way to get her.

The social interplay remained light and somewhat foolish. Now and then a couple would dance. At one point Ray suggested changing partners, but Gene quickly nixed that, and thankfully Rena agreed. "I'm not sharing my man with anybody. He's mine totally mine tonight!"

Her words were so obviously silly they had no real meaning, other than closing down Ray's suggestion.

Then she whispered softly to him: "And I can't wait to simply devour you!"

Gene whispered softly into her ear: "Thanks."

"Think nothing," she offered, so soft that he almost didn't hear the words, but certainly felt the soft warmth of her lips against his ear. "Just enjoy me."

All the others saw was a warm, intimate embrace which communicated all that was necessary.

"Well," Ray offered, "I'm for some real fun, then!"

"Like what?" Rena asked more to Gene than to the other man. She ran her hand down his chest. She whispered, softly, so only he could hear: "Ray has a whole bag of party games that end up with everybody stark and totally..." Her fingers gently clawed his arm.

Gene said: "Hey, no party games!"

92

"Why not?" Pat blurted out, as if disappointed. "Maybe games would be a good idea."

"No!" Gene snapped. "No way!"

That's all Pat needed to hear. "I'm for games!"

Strangely it was Rena who came to her defense with: "His kind of games are rather brutish!"

"Oh?" Pat sounded alarmed, glancing from Rena to Ray and back again.

"Believe me, his idea of a game would knock your eye-balls out, honey!"

"Really, now?" Pat shot back, biting on the bait.

"Wanna play Hide & Seek?" Rena inquired. "Have any idea of what is hidden to seek out?"

Pat blinked, uncertain.

Ray chuckled. "You know, babe, ya go into the meat market and you look at the deli and you start searching for the best damned sausage around!"

Rena cried out, laughingly: "Oh, shut up, Ray. You have no class!"

"Since when were you so picky, babe!" the man snapped, angrily.

Gene said: "Chill, Ray! Just do me a favor and chill!"

The man stared at him for a long moment, then shrugged.

"Thanks," Pat offered the air itself, with a deep sigh of relief.

That seemed to be a cue for a pounding to come from the front door. Everybody looked in that direction, shocked at the sudden, unexpected interruption.

"Who could that be?" Noel asked, not moving.

"You weren't expecting anybody?" Ray asked, trying to focus on the door.

Noel shook his head from side to side. "And I don't know anybody up here at the mountains."

"Somebody wanting directions from you?" June asked.

The man shook his head: "No—this is a dead end road; hardly anybody comes up this way."

"The police?" Ray suggested.

"Why?" Noel countered, starting to move toward the

door.

"Don't know, don't know. But it has to be some-body!" Ray cried out, throwing his hands in the air.

"There's only one way to find out," Noel laughed, looking back toward the others. "What's wrong with us? You'd think we were expecting the devil to be waiting on the other side! Can't be anything but a human face!"

The others laughed nervously back at him.

There was a scraping, metallic scratchy sound com-ing from the door, as if a key were struggling to fit in the lock.

Noel looked startled, puzzled, backed away, slightly.

Gene felt a fluttering in his stomach. He knew that there wasn't any reason to be feeling that way; and the only excuse he could give himself was that he'd had too much to drink. He looked toward Pat and then forced his attention back to Rena.

The door suddenly swung opened on it own, and strong breezes of cold air rushed into the room, followed by white flecks of snow.

They all looked at the opening in shock.

There was a man and woman standing there, looking at them, equally surprised. The man was holding an ugly gun in his right hand.

"Well, look at this!" the man announced, grinning, and eyes flowing over the women. "My, my—brother Noel is having an orgy!"

"Carl!" Noel managed to choke out, stepping back like a zombie.

The two newcomers moved into the room and the man closed the door. Then he turned and looked at every-body; one at a time—right into their eyes. Hard, hateful fury seethed in that stare. When he met Gene's eyes, it was like looking into the face of a madman. A shiver moved across his body.

Carl looked at the girl with him, then turned to Noel and said: "This is Helen. We thought we might come on up and spend a few quiet, intimate days here."

'When did you get out?" Noel demanded, his face turning hard, and almost white.

94

"Out? Why, that's no way to treat your brother. One would think that you weren't glad to see me. That's for sure." The man laughed hysterically. But his eyes remained cold.

There was silence and then Noel asked his question again. "When did you break jail?"

"Break jail?" Carl laughed nastily. "Why, they just let me out. Didn't you hear? I was such a nice guy that they opened the doors and said that I could leave."

"That's a lie!" Noel accused him. "You were sent in for life—without any chance of getting out!"

"Shut up—you shit!" Carl cried, swinging the back of his hand across Noel's face. Noel jerked stumbled and almost fell. Blood smeared across his lips.

Carl now swung the gun slowly back and forth. "Okay, just don't do anything cute!"

"You—" Noel started to say.

"Shut your goddamned mouth!" Carl commanded. "Now, tell me—which one is yours?"

"My what?"

"Girl. You know: chick. Lay. Woman! Whore. Whatever you call them now days?"

Noel didn't say anything. He just slowly got to his feet and looked angrily at his brother.

"I asked you a question!"

Pat stepped forward. "What do you want?"

Carl looked at her and his eyes stopped at the bulge of her breasts. Then he laughed and turned to Noel. "Well, well! So this is the broad you got such hot pants you bought her up here!" The man laughed, nastily. "Your secretary no doubt?"

"None of your damned business."

"What happened to the wifie? Is she still panting at your heels?"

"We're divorced," Noel admitted, angrily.

"So...she got wise and dumped you! Good for her!"

"Knock it off, Carl!"

The man's face hardened and his hand instinctively moved the gun in Noel's direction. "You just keep still! Got me, brother mine?"

There was a long silence. Gene felt the air tighten around him, fear clamping in his throat. It was taking several minutes to really mentally grasp the full implications of the exchange.

The gun. The reaction that Noel had to his brother's appearance. The statement about Carl having been sent up for life. That meant this was an escaped prisoner. And the gun could make him King.

More important was the frightening way the man fairly caressed Pat with his eyes. It had nothing, really, to do with beauty, but rather a power play between the two brothers. That put Pat in great danger.

A chill froze through Gene's spine.

"So you're the hot chickie-chickie!" Carl observed, stepping toward Pat.

She didn't move, or even seem to cringe as he stopped in front of her. "What kind of kisses you been giving brother Noel? I bet they ain't so blah as his! I bet that much."

"Don't. You. Dare. Touch me!" she said in a tight even voice.

"You got balls!" Carl laughed. "Real balls!" But his eyes were feasting on her body and neckline. "Real big... balls!"

He laughed again, hyena fashion. His left hand, reached out towards her.

She backed away: "Don't even think about it!"

Surprise showed on his face. His eyes swept once more down her body. Greedily so.

"You kidding?" he finally asked, his voice slightly touched with humor. "You gotta be shakin' my leg!"

"Don't touch me!" she repeated in a thin voice, as if those were the only words she knew.

"I'll do what I damn please!" he told her very quietly. But he moved back a few steps, then turned and looked at each person in the room. "I do as I please to everybody here. You got me?"

"By what authority," Ray demanded, "do you come in here and start bullying us?"

Carl moved like he'd been propelled by rocket fuel. Nobody had a chance to stop him or even guess what he was

96

about to do. Without a word he slashed the barrel of his gun across Ray's boyish face. A jagged bloody crease appeared. A scream sounded from June, who stepped away, her forearm covering her mouth, her eyes wide in terror and horror.

"By that authority!" Carl announced in a calm voice. "By authority of this little old gun of mine!"

He moved across the room, toward the bar.

"You know," he said in an almost pleasant voice, "I think that it's about time the party continued. I really could use a drink."

Noel finally recovered from his first daze. He moved over to where his brother was pouring a drink for himself.

"Just what have you gotten yourself into this time?"

Carl looked up, his dark features frowning a little. "Just what do you mean by that, big brother?"

"Exactly what I said!"

Carl smiled and turned toward Helen. "Think we should tell them? Confess all. So they're in on the whole thing. What do you think, sweetie?"

The woman seemed to cringe just a little, drawing in on herself, in alarm. Then she moved to his side and leaned close, an expression of very real fear crossed her face. "No—don't say anything! Please!"

"Why not? It doesn't really matter, anyway." The man shrugged, then downed the drink in his hand. "They all might as well know what they are going to die for."

He let a dramatic silence fall on the room, grinning insanely as he examined the reactions of the others to his statement. "Of course you knew that—didn't you?"

"You can't mean that!" Noel exclaimed in horror.

"Of course I do," Carl said in very cold, casual manner. "Look at you. Look at you all!"

He turned to Helen. "Look at them. Scared to death. I won't even have to kill them. They'll kill themselves with fear."

He laughed this time in great pleasure at his quick wit.

"You can't mean it!" Noel said again, his face white and tense.

"Well, now, brother—let's say I can mean it and then

we might say that I don't. I'll just let you figure it out. Think about it—all of you!" He raised the gun above his head. "I've already killed three people today—think a few others won't make a bit of difference?"

Helen looked at him in a strange way. "Three?"

"Three!" Carl looked nervously at her. "Two—I'm...a little confused and tired from the bump on my head. But what difference does it make? Two, three, or nine? I can fry for one as quickly as a hundred!"

He examined Noel again. "So you figure it out, Big Bro. We did a bank job that will make us rich. And Helen and me are heading out of the country after it all blows over. So you figure it out! Do I want to leave behind a bunch of creeps just dying to turn us in?"

The man laughed, throwing his head back slightly. "I figure, let 'em do their dyin' before I leave. Best that way, now don't you all think so?"

The silence that met his words was heavy, hard.

"Fine. Okay. Well, I'll be a sport about all this. If you all are nice folk, I'll consider returning the favor. I promise I won't make it hurt...much! If you're all nice to me!"

Helen hugged to him, a bit frightened looking. "Is it necessary, Carl. Can't we..."

"Oh, sure, babe. Why not be generous. Why not even share the money with these dead heads? Would that make you happy? Make them full partners, so they can't yak, yak it up with the authorities."

He looked at the others, "You see my problem, now don't you?"

98

ACT FIVE

ANY ONE CAN DIE! BY CHARLES NUETZEL

XVIII.

THE TERROR PLAY BEGINS

Pat sat in the chair, her arms supporting her chin. Several hours had past since Carl Anderson and Helen had joined them. Hours which had turned a frustrating evening into one filled with terror. They were all depressively quite, locked in their own inner world of personal fear. June had cared for Ray's bleeding face which was more ugly than seriously damaged.

Carl and Helen seemed to be working out some plans, very quietly at the bar. The man continually pawed her, rather crudely, laughing from time to time, apparently oblivious to the others there in the room.

Nobody dared to challenge the man's dictates. He had warned them in a very cold manner to just stay put, and not to be wandering around without checking with him first. The moment any of the did make a move from where they were, he's eyes popped up, noted them, then he nodded as if handing out permission to school kids.

Pat saw all this with a continually sick feeling. Somebody had to do something.

She found it impossible to avoid Gene any more. What was the use? Games were over.

The thoughts that had been racing through her mind had exposed a dramatic changed in her feelings for Gene. The threat of death striking them down cut though all the crap. People lived by rules that were silly and foolish; crushing their real needs, dreams, and hopes through prideful loops that stopped them at every turn. Suddenly she only regretted having screwed up her life so badly. Now. Too late, she wanted a second chance. It was ironic how a person's ideas changed so quickly. The death threat made everything focused, hard. What one thought important before, turned pale. All those petty beliefs, against grabbing life to the fullest, just didn't count anymore.

She looked up at Gene. They had not been avoiding one another since Carl had arrived. Even if they hadn't exchanged a word. The eye contact was now quite penetrating, exposing raw nerves, raw feelings, honest concern. Yet they still seemed guarded, afraid to reveal too much to the others.

So much had taken place in the last twenty-four hours that she still felt dizzy from the effects.

"Gene," she whispered, motioning him over.

Carl's eyes lifted, noted her for a moment, but he said nothing, returning his attention to Helen, as Gene moved to Pat's side.

As Gene looked down at her, his gaze reflected her own longing. She wanted to tell him that it had all been a mistake—that they should never have broken up. But the words wouldn't come. They choked in her throat and stayed there.

"Gene—what are we going to do?" she finally managed, looking away, taking in the room.

"Nothing—just wait," was the man's carefully stated reply.

Ice settled in her stomach. There it was again: Gene's inability to take action. How many times in the past had he come so close to sweeping her off her feet, then suddenly chickened out, backing off like an inexperienced school-boy. It was a pattern of non-action. The guy was just a kid in a man's body. And something of an idealistic fool!

She looked at him again, and suddenly realized that what he said was probably right: what else was there to do?

But she resented the man's logically set mind.

"We can't just sit around and wait for him to kill us!" she almost hissed between clinched teeth, frightened her words would reach the madman at the bar.

"I know."

102

"We *must* do…something!"

The conversation hung there because Carl suddenly stood, his eyes looking coldly at her. She felt an uncomfortable burn creep over her under his gaze. Those eyes fairly sucked in her image like he was some wild beast about to leap on its mate.

"What are you two talking about?" he demanded, coming to a halt before them.

"Nothing," Gene said simply, avoiding the man's eyes.

"I just bet," Carl laughed, sneeringly. "I bet you wonder what I'm going to do with you. Will I really start whacking you off, one at a time? Which is first to go? You? Her? Maybe them over there?" The man pointed behind him at the others. "I bet that's what you're doing! Ain't it? Just wondering. Well, that's a good idea. Keep you bright and alert."

They didn't say anything to that; both just stayed in the position they had been in when he had walked up.

"I think I asked you a question!'"

Noel moved to his brother's side. "Leave them alone."

"What business is it of yours?" Carl demanded, without even turning to face his brother.

For a moment it looked as if Noel could easily attack him. But, instead, the man simply announced, rather stiffly: "They're guests of mine!"

At least, Pat thought, *he's got guts! Guts enough to stand up to his brother.*

"So—so they're your guests!" Carl remarked, smiling. "So, are you gonna play the big hero and save them from...from whatever I fate is in store…at my nasty hands? You got the guts to do that, Big Bro?"

Silence answered him.

"I thought so. All huffity bluff, aren't you, dear brother? Dear big brother who made all the money—got all the breaks, while his younger brother had to take it on the chin. Dear brother who married my woman."

"She wanted me!" Noel retorted, defensively.

"Shit, she wanted your money. What else would a

man like you have to give a woman like her?"

"Come on, Carl," Noel soothed, as if somehow it might be possible to keep him under control. "Let's not flash the family dirt in public."

"Oh, boy. You got the nerve! You sure do!" Carl exploded, whipping around and facing him. "Some nerve, I must say. All things considered. She was smart to kick you out! Only thing smart she did, after dumping me! For you! Crap!"

Noel looked savagely near losing it, then backed away from the smaller man, who immediately laughed at that.

"You're a no good sniveling bastard. And oh so proper middle class bum! You make me sick. You always did! Everybody favored you! What dumb fools! Class, my ass. You just took, took, took, got the advantages. Well, things changed, bro, Big Bad Bro. I got bigger and you...you're just a silly damned social climbing bastard whose luck just hit the dump!"

The man turned and walked back to Helen.

"Ya got no class!" he raged, grabbing the woman and pushing her out in front of him. "This lady has class, she has. Planned the whole thing. Helped me when I was unconscious." He tapped his forehead where a bruised small lump showed. "Damned if she don't have class. Not like you...bums!"

Carl laughed and then embraced Helen from behind, letting his arm encase her breasts in a rather crude manner. "She's my classy little assy, she sure is!"

"I'm sorry," Noel told Pat and Gene. "Somehow I'll get you folks out of this mess."

"Yeah, folks, hear the Big Man! Brother mine is gonna get ya all out of this Big Bad Mess. He sure is!"

Carl turned to the bar again. He picked up a bottle and raised it to his lips, taking several large gulps. Then he turned and looked at the solemn group.

Ray and June were sitting on the sofa, near the fireplace. Rena was standing before the fire, looking at the floor. Pat and Gene were where they'd been before, every once in awhile glancing at each other.

104

"Hell. You folks are dull company. What kind of party is this?" Carl demanded. "A dead one?" He laughed at that, added: "Soon to be, sooner than necessary if things don't pick up fast!"

He gave them a mocking wink and looked towards the door that led to a bedroom. "At least *we* have something to celebrate!"

She didn't smile at him, but merely said: "You can't mean it!"

"What," he snapped, eyes narrowing.

"You know," she almost whispered the words. "Do what you said to them. There's got to be…a better way."

"Goddamn bitch, cram it!" Carl screamed, slapping her face. "This is a party! A happy party!"

Silence met his announcement.

He gulped from the bottle and then moved to the stereo in the corner of the room. "A radio—that's what we need. Considering no TV or cable up here! Maybe we'll get some news about how the police are taking our little caper. That would be interesting—now, wouldn't it?"

It took just a second for turn the radio on, and then Carl played with the dial until he finally found a station he had been looking for. There was only music playing. Nervously he looked at his watch and then grinned. "It won't be long until the news comes on. They should mention something about what happened—with the Doc and all that. They're sure to say something!"

He sounded like a proud celebrity about to read his reviews in the papers on opening night.

The others were silent. Pat felt ill inside; a nervous fear that had more to do with her hating herself. She thought about Gene and herself; about their good times together—and the weeks they had missed out on. If she'd gone off and gotten married to him they'd probably be safe somewhere on a honeymoon right at that moment. A part of her had loved him, for sure, but another side found his conventional idealism some what of a bore. She had wanted full thrills in life. Too young to die without having lived a little. Well, she was getting a lifetime full of thrills this evening, and wanted nothing to do with them.

Pat felt confused about everything. She had dumped Gene to open her life to a more exciting possible future with other men. And instead she'd moped depressed and lonely, and ended up in a bar drinking by herself, then into jail on a DUI and now all this. None of it made sense. If she'd wanted thrills, she sure as hell had gone about it all in the wrong way. And look where it had gotten her!

If only she'd accepted Gene's proposal. How different things would be.

She would have never gone out with Noel. Never been here to cross paths with the man's brother; a crazed killer.

She looked up at Gene and wanted to be held in his strong arms. But it was too late.

"*The news!*" Carl suddenly shouted. "Now you'll all see what a big man I am. Yes, brother Noel you'll see how big your brother Carl has become."

"...and third man, a doctor, was found brutally murdered in his home this evening. They believe that it was connected with the bank yesterday. The direction of the flight, indicated by the report of Mr. Terrington, whose car was robbed earlier this morning, would show a direct line to the mountains. All roads are being blocked in the hope of making a quick capture. The state police seem quite confident and have announced that from the way those three had been brutally murdered that Carl Anderson, an escaped convict, was the killer.... And now the weather...."

Carl flipped the radio off and turned to the others, his eyes wide with excitement. "Didn't I tell you I was famous? They can recognize my style!"

"That's nothing, Carl," Noel said dryly.

"What do you mean it's nothing? What the damned hell do—"

"Please cut out the swearing; there are ladies around—"

106

"Go to hell! You ain't my mother no more! You ain't nothing. Just a goddamn bastard slob that got everything—and left me nothing! That's all you are. But now I got everything." He waved the gun which he had held in his hand every moment since he had arrived. "And I got all the money! That's what I got!" He reached for the bottle of whiskey which was now half empty. "And I got me my woman!"

"You better lay off," Helen warned him, carefully touching his arm and looking up into his eyes. "You can't afford to get drunk!"

He laughed. "I got you here, baby, to watch over me!" He handed her the gun. "You watch these slobs. It only takes a woman to watch them. They aren't going to do nothing! Nothing at all!"

Pat couldn't imagine what kept Helen from turning the gun in the man's direction and blowing his guts out, after what he'd done to her earlier.

But then, she realized, *one could never tell about a woman's feelings toward her man. She might take anything he offered!*

Pat felt a shiver run through her as she looked at the others. Everybody was scared to make a move; afraid to take a chance of rubbing Carl in the wrong direction—all but Noel; but that was different. The man knew his own brother and no doubt just how far he could push the man.

She felt a hand touch her shoulder and turned to see Gene looking down at her. She tried to smile, but it did no good; she was scared and didn't mind showing it.

Carl looked in her direction and a chuckle sounded from his lips. Then his eyes moved toward Rena. A knowing expression crossed his features.

"You're Rena, aren't you?" he asked. "Gene-boy's squeeze!"

The bleached blonde just looked blankly at him. Then she slowly nodded.

"You have a good time with Genie-boy?" he demanded, then not waiting for an answer added, shaking his head sadly from side to side, "But I sure bet he had a hot time, though. You look like one lush dish, a lunch, dinner and morning snake all spread out onto one plate, beggin' to be eaten alive!"

Carl's eyes feasted on her body, openly admiring every curve. "Bet you're a really hot dish! Blazing chili peppers alive! Even hotter than you look. And you look like a furnace about to explode! Right out of that tight dress!"

He winked and then nodded. "Well, I love that name. Rena...bet you know how to pleasure a man real good—don't you?" He laughed, then drunkenly moved to her. "It's about time for a big hot meal. This is the dullest party I've seen. And I'm hungry!"

He stopped before Rena. Then his hand leaped out and wrapped around her neck. He yanked her face to his, powerfully forcing her lips against his mouth. Rena didn't struggle; she was too smart for that. But she didn't respond, either.

Angrily, Carl pushed her away. He looked at Helen and then moved to her, taking the gun. "I think we'll just have a little fun! How about it, brother Noel—you have some jazzy CDs up here?"

Noel just shrugged.

"Okay—I got a great idea. We'll put them on and let the girls do a little fun dancing for us ... a, well, call it a strip show! Right down to the raw. All of them. A real hot strip show! What do ya think, man?"

"Come on, leave them alone!" Noel objected, tensing, arching towards his brother.

"Zip!" Carl growled. "It up! Bring on the band. And you nice ladies start dancin' away your civvies. I wanna see some naked flesh strutting hot stuff for us men to drool over. What do ya say, boys?"

He didn't wait for their stunned response. "That's gonna heat things up a bit. And remember girls. This is a Contest! The best stripper gets the prize!"

He merely chuckled at that, waving the gun at Noel, who only hesitated moment. "Music Master!" Then to the ladies: "Ya can start the show any time you like—as long as it's immediately. Dance for your lives!"

108

XIX.

YOU WANT TO DIE?

Gene couldn't believe his ears when Carl made his announcement. At first he thought that the man was just kidding. He must be kidding. No one other than a brute would have made such a demand—no one but a madman.

"You can't do that!" he objected, stepping forward, feeling the fury which had been building up in him suddenly surge outwards.

Carl just froze. Then slowly he turned and looked at Gene.

"What's that you said?" he demanded, stepping toward Gene. "What's that you said about me not being able to do something?"

For some reason Gene wasn't afraid; he was too mad to be afraid, "You can't do that!"

"You got the balls to stop me?" Carl laughed.

It was an ugly laugh that shattered through the room, resounding on each wall. Then it slowly faded out and his eyes squinted. "You know there, hero-man, I really was just joking a bit. Just joking—before. Now I think I'll do that. Why not?" He moved, his face suddenly close to Gene's. "See what that big mouth of yours has gotten you into? See, big mouth? And no balls!"

Gene felt a tightness claw at his stomach; then the tense hurt became abruptly a jarring pain that doubled him over. The wind whipped from his lungs and he felt himself stumbling. Somewhere in the back of his mind he realized that Carl had rammed the gun into his stomach. Slowly in gasps the air started returning to his lungs. Then his vision sharpened and he focused on Carl's handsome features. They were leering at him.

"I could have just squeezed the trigger! That easy and you're guts would be spread out all over the place!"

Gene's fists tightened and he took a threatening step forward. Much to his surprise he walked right into Pat who had moved between them.

"Don't, Gene. I think he'd kill you!"

"Come on, hero-man!" Carl taunted. "Let me see your balls, man! Come and get it. I'm ready for ya. Wanna take over? Take me on. I'll put the gun down and we can do it man to man! Show you're honey there what you are made of."

"Don't, Gene. It isn't worth it!" Pat begged, pushing him back.

There was a long silence while Carl still held the gun pointed at Gene. His face was eager and bright with excitement. He was just waiting for one false move; one step in his direction.

"What's wrong, lover-boy? Don't you want to take me on?"

Pat's hand braced against him. She looked really frightened.

"Come on get it, big meat man!" Carl challenged. "Promise, I'll put the gun down and make it a fair fight."

Noel warned, behind his brother's back, silently shaking his head.

"I'm all yours!" Carl mocked him. "Take me, little boy, I'm yours!" He laughed hysterically. "He'd make some catch in the joint! They'd whack him right up hard day and night. And he wouldn't do a damn thing about it but whimper! Right? Whimpering love-mate of the cell block! No fun at all!"

Pat again pressed her hand on his chest in silent plead.

"Okay. We got things straight?" Carl demanded, turning his back on them, facing the others.

Gene sobered; the hate and fury still burned through

110

him, but the reality held him back. The man might kill him sooner or later, but where there was life there was still the chance of getting out of this mess alive.

"Balls boy, ain't you gonna jump me while my back is turned? I dare you!" Carl laughed and lowered the gun's point to the floor. Without even turning to them, he said: "So look at the hero-man. Just look at him, shivering and quaking."

"Calm down, Carl," Helen suggested in a carefully shaded voice.

There was a silence and then Carl turned, stared at Pat, and smiled quite charmingly. "Look how she came to his defense. Did you see the expression in her eyes?" He looked at his brother. "That the kind of woman you run around with. Somebody else's broad!"

He laughed again and then stepped to the middle of the room. He looked at Rena, his eyes examining her in a most greedy and hungry manner. "Yeah, I was talking something about having you do a peep show for us—when that white-faced slob interrupted me. Anybody else have any objections?"

Silence met his words. He grinned and chuckled. "Helen—won't that be a ball? Let the women do a strip show. A real honest to goodness strip show!"

"Sure. Sure," Helen answered in a tired voice. "Sure, honey. Some distraction, right?"

"You got it, babe! Start the music and let the show begin!"

Moving to the CD player, he turned it on.

"You know, my friends, I haven't been to a real live strip show since I was penned up a year ago."

He glanced up at them, smiling. "I think that Rena here must know a little about such things—don't you, doll?"

Rena didn't say anything, but the expression of fright in her eyes told all there was to say.

Gene felt sick inside, but he realized how useless it was to attempt to interfere. This simply was not worth dying for. Pat had been right about that; it wasn't worth it. So the girls dance naked. That wouldn't kill them—and there was the slim chance Carl might get distracted by their erotic dis-

111

play.

Somehow they had to find a chance to overpower the man. They couldn't die without a fight.

And it was obvious the man intended to kill them. And that was all that counted.

Slowly Carl turned. "Well, now. Let's see what kind of hot dance you can show us, Rena girl! I sure wanna see all you got to offer." He leered at her, smiling crookedly. "All of you, simply show me all of you. A wiggle here and a wiggle there!" He patted his chest, then his groin, laughing. "Drag 'em out and give me all the wiggle ya got, sexy babe! I wanna see you're boobies dancin' and prancin' wiggle, waggle."

Noel started to step forward. "You must be kidding—don't do this, Carl!"

"Shut up!" The man's eyes didn't even move from Rena.

"You can't make her do it!" Noel objected again, moving closer to his brother.

"Zip your lip!—don't think I wouldn't plug you just as fast as anybody else in this room. Maybe faster! So zip your mouth. And watch the hot show!"

Noel moved back, shock showing in his face. His lips whitened a little and his eyes dropped to the floor.

"Okay, now. Show time!" Carl demanded, looking at Rena.

Gene felt sick inside; he wanted to do something—anything—to stop this raw display of Rena's body. Last night he'd just thought of her as a tramp—now he felt horror for her. He looked at Rena, and for a second her eyes flashed toward him. They weren't the eyes of the brazen little tramp but those of a woman who is frightened for her life.

"Come on, hot chili! Get red hot for me!" Carl exclaimed as music sounded from the speakers. It was heavy with a solid beat; not rock and roll, but a more rhythmic jazz number with a blues flavor. "Come on, baby, let's see your bouncin' boobs!"

A sigh passed Rena's lips and her eyes moved from person to person in the room.

"Please, mister!" she begged. But the tone in her

voice was hopeless.

"Don't be bashful; we're all friends!" Carl laughed, looking anxiously at the full, large crevice between her breasts which showed off almost nakedly already against her dress. "Hell, you're all but naked at the tits anyway. What do you care if we really see all you got? You women always wanna tease a man nuts! Start teasin'! And now! I wanna see your tease machine!"

A nervous snicker sounded from Helen, and Gene looked momentarily in her direction. She was smiling and her eyes were brightly eager.

"Please," Rena said in a small voice. She just stood there like a lost child, hands at her side.

Carl slowly moved the gun up in her direction, pointing it at her belly. "You want to die? The hard way?"

That last made him chuckle. "Can you imagine her dying like that...the hard way!" Again he laughed at his own crude humor. "Make it hot, babe! Dance for you life! You don't wanna die in agonized pain with a hole in your belly, now do you?"

Rena shook her head from side to side.

"Okay—then! Get going! I simply can't take no more of this damned teasing!"

Rena's face was deathly white, her eyes and her lips set almost in a thin line. She looked down at the floor, helplessly.

"Come on! Come on. The show must go on!" Carl snapped. "And this is your big break! Gotta win the contest! Cause who knows what the booby prize will be?"

He laughed hysterical at that. "I get all the boobies! Anyway...do your bump and grind!"

"I don't know how" she mumbled in a shaking voice.

"Sure you do. Just take it off, take it off! The dress, honey bunny! Let's see what you really have to offer!" He motioned impatiently with his gun. "We don't have all day! This is a contest, remember. And there's other girls anxious to offer up their act for the Big Prize!"

Gene felt the tightness in his guts, he didn't dare do anything but sit there and watch Carl slowly undress Rena with his commands.

113

Rena's fingers moved up to the top of her dress and started to pull the straps downwards and then slip her arms out of them. She reluctantly let the cloth creep down off her breasts.

Her fingers paused, almost pleading for him to let her quit. But of course that was impossible.

"Come on! Come on! You've only just begun!"

Rena looked at the gun which was still leveled at her stomach. A choking sounded from her throat, and her hands instinctively went to her mouth.

"Come on! The woman who gives the best show might be saved from a fate worse than death!" Carl laughed at that and then leaned forward. "Now, that's a good idea. The woman that puts on a good show doesn't have to worry about another—more private one!" he laughed again. "Come—give it a little swing! Make them boobs really rock and roll! More bounce to the ounce!"

Rena started to sway to the music.

"Come on, baby, start dumping the dress! I wanna see your heart and soul! All a blaze! Down with the dress!"

Her fingers began moving the dress downwards over her voluptuous body. To her waist, then past her hips and then finally falling in a circle around her feet.

She came to a stop and looked blankly at Carl; hate was showing in her face and eyes.

"Take it off! Take it off!" Carl screamed, gasping between drunken laughs. "Gotta see your lovely...heart!"

For the first time Gene saw just how drunk the man was. Up to this moment he hadn't known how badly the liquor had affected Carl; the man held his drinks well—but the expression in his glazed eyes was quite revealing.

Now was his chance to jump the bastard. That thought left him numb with surprise, because he hadn't consciously been aware that he'd made a decision to act. What chance did they have? Yet his mind had been waiting for the right moment. And now seemed the right moment, while Carl's attention was on Rena.

Just then Ray leaped forward, his face distorted with rage, the bloody bruised cut across his cheek making him have the look of a savage animal. Nobody had paid any at-

114

tention to him up until now.

Carl didn't even seem to move his eyes away from Rena's now nude body. His handed shifted in position, pointing the gun in Ray's direction, and his fingers squeezed. "Keep dancin', babe!"

ANY ONE CAN DIE! BY CHARLES NUETZEL

XX.

DEAD OR ALIVE

The city police had put out an all points call for the capture of Carl Anderson, notifying the authorities in every small town within three hundred miles of the murder of Doctor Landers, the man Carl had killed earlier that day.

It was the slow careful work of a team of detectives to decide in which direction the man's flight had taken. And every indication pointed toward the mountains. And the first place to look was the resort which speckled the large lake.

"Search every cabin. Every room. And for God's sake be careful, because this man has nothing to lose by killing you. He's set for the chair—the moment he escaped that was the only direction he could have gone. Get him—dead or alive," were the orders.

The only thing that held up the search was the storm which had by now blocked all roads. But they knew one thing; if Carl Anderson was up at the resort lake in one of the cabins, he was snowed in. If they couldn't get to him he couldn't get out.

But this lonely team had another worry. How could they really be sure that he was up there? Maybe they were wasting their time. So they moved carefully and waited calmly. There wasn't any hurry or rush. If their man was there, he wouldn't be going anyplace. They had plenty of time. One way or another they'd get their man—but they hoped it would be before another person was killed.

Any One Can Die! by Charles Nuetzel

XXI.

SEARCH FOR SURVIVAL

Pat looked horrified at the dead body of Ray. it happened so fast that she could hardly believe her eyes.

Rena stood there, naked, but mouth open as if to scream, but no sound coming out.

Carl Anderson didn't seem to react to what he had done. He wasn't even looking at the still, lifeless form of Ray. It was as if he had killed some kind of bug.

Chills ran over her spine and she looked up at Gene who was standing tense and white next to her.

Thank God, she thought, *it hadn't been Gene!*

Slowly Carl's eyes moved in the direction of the dead man. He smiled slightly and then stood and stepped over to him. "See what happens to a man who tries to jump Carl Anderson? See?"

He examined each person. Then his foot suddenly kicked out, smashing at the dead face, snapping it backwards.

Pat felt acid race up her throat and then she doubled over, coughing in her lap.

Her shoulders were raised by strong hands and she felt the tender pressure of Gene's body comforting her.

"You people are party poops!" Carl cursed, turning off the CD. "I think I have a much better idea. A lot more fun than just sitting out here looking at a woman do nothing but be scared." Strangely his voice was even and frighteningly sober sounding, as if the killing had excited him more

119

than Rita's naked body. He looked at her and then laughed. "You didn't put on such a good show—know that, baby? You know that, don't you. A nothing show. But you sure have a body! Love them boobs!"

Without looking in Helen's direction he threw the gun to her. "Watch these people, while I have some fun with this girl with big tits!"

He grabbed Rena's arm and jerked her toward the bedroom. "I think it's about time that some real fun happened! You just won the Big Prize!"

Gene tensed against Pat, but she held him back. Over his shoulder she saw Noel go white yet he didn't move to attempt to stop his brother. It would be useless and everybody knew it

She looked at Helen and was surprised to see the strange expression on the woman s face It was a mixture of hate and excitement

What kind of woman would sit quietly back and let her man go into bed with another one? Pat wondered. She'd never be able to stand it

Yet Gene had been making it with Rena That much she was sure of; and here she was, clutched in his arms. And that was a strange thing. They'd seemed to have broken past the barrier of pride.

Finally gaining control of herself, she looked up at Gene. They gazed at each other for a long time without saying a word. It was just like it had been before they had broken up. But now it was too late to do anything about it. They'd probably end up dead like Ray.

"Okay, you men," Helen's voice broke the silence, "How about getting this dead guy out of here!"

"Where?" Noel asked stupidly, as if coming out of a shocked daze.

"I don't know! You're the one that owns this place. Out on the back porch for all I care!"

Noel looked at Gene and for a moment neither did anything.

A sob sounded from June who had stood frozen. Now she turned her head and hid it against the wall.

"Come on, you guys! Let's get this dead body out of

here!" Helen ordered again, motioning with the gun.

Pat thought she heard a slight edge of fear in the other woman's voice, but she wasn't sure. Maybe it had been anger. Hope moved through her as she thought of the possibility that Helen might really be furious about what was taking place in the other room. Maybe if they could turn her against Carl. Maybe that was a hope; a chance.

She didn't know; but if she could start to eat away on that point with Helen, maybe it would be possible to get a way out—somehow save all their lives. Desperation made anything possible! After all, a woman was a woman; no matter how cold she might be. Pat felt that it quite possible to dig down into the womanly ways of Helen and hit pay dirt. It was worth a try. And that might be all they had.

* * * * * *

Gene just numbed as he watched events happen: first he saw Ray jerk backwards and fall to the floor under the impact of Carl's bullet. Then the man had kicked his friend's dead face. Pat got sick; and then the forcing of Rena into the bedroom, alone, was almost too much.

Then Helen with the gun. Maybe she wouldn't be so quick to kill a person. But he wasn't about to take any chances.

Then came the command to get rid of the body.

Noel finally shrugged and Gene moved with him to Ray's dead form.

"Where?" Gene asked.

"The kitchen—maybe out in the back porch."

The two of them lifted Ray from the floor and started for the small kitchen The swinging door moved shut behind them and then Noel turned and looked at Gene.

"We have to do something—he's going to kill all of us!"

"I know," Gene said in a tense voice, trying to think of anything that might be done.

Noel released the body, letting Gene hold it upright, as he looked at the back door. He returned a second later. "We're snowed in. The back porch; that's the only place."

121

It was funny, Gene thought as they dropped Ray's body on the floor of the service porch, *how a person could get used to violence.*

He wasn't used to it so much as he was numb.

Ray, a good friend, had just been shot, but he couldn't help feeling a sense of relief because it could have been himself lying there on the cold floor. It had been too close.

"What are we going to do?" Noel said, almost to himself, looking at the far wall.

"Maybe we can overpower Helen. After all, there are two of us—and we're supposed to be healthy men...and only one of her—"

"But with a gun."

The two of them were silent for a moment and then Noel slowly shook his head from side to side.

"I feel terrible about this. It's all my fault," Noel groaned.

"Don't be silly! It just happened—and somehow we gotta keep our heads and get out of this."

Helen's voice sounded through the door. "What's keeping you two?"

"We'd better return," Noel remarked moving toward the front room. "If she knew we were talking about—"

"Okay—we'll think of something."

It wasn't until they were in the other room that Gene realized what a chance they'd missed getting a weapon. The kitchen surely had knives.

Damned fools! He cursed. *Maybe later.*

122

ACT SIX

Any One Can Die! by Charles Nuetzel

XXII.

RAPE SCENE

When Carl pulled Rena into the bedroom he felt a nervous dig of excitement run through his body. Rena was one of those sexy little tramps that he really liked. The moment he had seen her earlier, when he and Helen had arrived at the cabin, he had been anxious to see that body under the tight-fitting dress. Now he knew. And it was better than he'd imagined possible. The woman really took care of herself.

"Okay, baby—you know what I want!" he told Rena. "On the bed. Make a fuss and you'll get your brains batted in. Play like you like me and maybe you will enjoy what I'll give you. You won't be the first that I made crazy with it!"

He gave her a push toward the bed.

Rena didn't say anything, but quietly lay on the bed stretching her body full length as she obviously imagined he wanted.

'That's it, baby! I sure like what you're offering!" Carl looked down at her and grinned crookedly. "You got a real body, I'll say that much for you. Those boobs just stand at attention!"

"Christ," she moaned in a shaking voice.

"I ain't him. But you'll sure be screaming his name before we're finished. I promise you, you'll enjoy!"

"Don't bet on it!" she said so softly that he almost didn't hear her.

"Take it easy, baby. I want to enjoy this. Just relax. I don't want you tense in the wrong places, now do I? There's

125

no hurry. We got all the time in the world." It was as if he hadn't heard her.

He continued to look at her body, her white throbbing throat. And he couldn't help thinking that she was beginning to react under his eagerly heated gaze. He'd make her enjoy it.

Grinning, Carl said, "You and me, babe, are going to know sin city! And you're gonna scream for more and more. Cause I know how to sin! And you sure as hell know how to enjoy us sinners! I bet you've had your fill of them! Oh, you're really something to feast on!"

He chuckled, quickly stripping. Strutting around the room, eyes locked on her lush body, he laughed: "See what I have for you?"

Finally he moved down to her side and ran his hand along her arm. She squirmed under the touch and he laughed. "You like it—don't you? Now admit it. I'm some hard hunk and you're just the soft body ...."

His voice lingered in mid-air as his fingers played along her flesh, down over her nipples, then lower across her belly. "What soft flesh you have."

Biting her lip, Rena didn't move, scared to say or do anything.

"You look frightened!" he chuckled, taking her hand in his. Surprisingly tender, he stroked it almost thoughtfully. "Don't be frightened. I ain't got nothing you ain't seen or had before. Only I'm better than most. I know how to really please a lady. Oh, believe me. I do!"

She shivered, and he guessed that wasn't from desire.

"Really, baby, you'll just love what I have to give you! My number one prize possession will soon be all yours!"

Carl laughed tauntingly and then started to slide his hand downwards toward her stomach.

Yes, he thought, *this was the kind of woman he really went for.* He really liked what he saw, and felt.

"Now its your turn. Show me the wonder of your lips ...you have such beautiful lips. I wonder what they feel like. Come on...show me how gentle and loving they can be on my Big Prize!"

126

He took her head in his strong hands and urged it down to where he wanted those lips to be. "Take it all, baby! Take it all!"

ANY ONE CAN DIE! BY CHARLES NUETZEL

XXIII.

DANGER PLAY

The moment that the two men left Pat and Helen alone, Pat turned to the other woman, looking at her for a long time, and then she said: "How can you stand that?"

"What?"

"Him in there with her?"

"Oh, that?" A queer expression crossed Helen's features, and her eyes flashed in that direction.

Pat offered, rather tensely: "I wouldn't let my man do a thing like that with another woman."

"What difference does it make? Just as long as he comes back to little old Helen."

"I think he's just using you. I don't think he gives a damn about you. Any man who treats a woman like he does you just doesn't care."

The expression clouded Helen's features, just the eyes, seemed to show a moment of flashing hurt. Then she relaxed. "Don't be silly."

"Silly or not…he doesn't give a bloody damn about anything or body but himself."

She frowned, shook her head. "He's my man!"

"And any other woman's man! He doesn't care who he gets into! What kind of man is that?"

Helen look angry, and simply said: "Get off my back, will you!"

"Oh come on. You don't fool me. He's just got you twisted around his fingers. He can do what he wants to you.

Hit you. Kick you around. Take you to bed. Shove you aside for another woman. He's just using you," Pat continued, following up her attack.

"Shut up, you!" Helen snarled, pointing the gun threateningly at Pat. "Shut up—you little…snob! What kind of woman are you? I bet you ain't even had a man in you. Not a real man, like Carl, anyway. So shut your damned mouth! You have no idea how great he is! Best a girl could ever have! Believe me, you'll be surprised when it is your turn in there with him! I promise you…"

The woman frowned at that point, then bit her lower lip. "Oh, shut up!"

Pat smiled to herself, because she'd hit pay dirt. Helen was truly annoyed at what was happening, and had exposed her real feeling in that angry retort. In a way Pat felt sorry for her. That kind of trap was the worst kind. Doing anything to keep her man.

Or was it?

Pat paused in her thoughts, remembering what kind of trap she and Gene had gotten themselves into. Just the opposite one!

It was silly, now that she thought of it. They had both been just a couple of grown-up kids. Adults in body; but not in mind. She had developed woman's breasts, but not a woman's emotional maturity. Instead of running when Gene wanted to marry her, she should have gone into his arms.

At least Helen was sticking to her man—regardless of what he did. Maybe he was in the wrong kind of business; but she had backed him. She loved him and took whatever he handed out. Cause he was her man.

Pat had run from her man. If they got out of this, she was going to try to start over with Gene—if he would have her. That much she knew

Helen's voice interrupted her thoughts.

"What's keeping you two?" she called through the kitchen door.

A moment later Gene and Noel joined them.

The next hour went slowly for Pat, because of what was going on in the next room and the fact that nobody could do anything to stop it. She and June sat on the sofa, next to

130

each other, while Noel and Gene were seated at the bar, lost in quiet conversation.

Only Helen was alone, a large glass of whiskey next to her, where she waited in a large leather covered chair in the far corner of the room.

The low moans and grunts that whispered from behind the closed door said far more than anybody wanted to know. It almost sounded as if Rena were actually enjoying what Carl was doing. Of course that had to be impossible!

Every once in a while, Helen glanced angrily at door to the bedroom. Every so often they could hear louder moans but nothing else. Neither Rena nor Carl came out. Then there was a low sobbing and a sudden scream followed by more sobbing and then quiet.

The minutes dragged.

Pat looked at her watch and was shocked to see how late it was. Early morning: 4:00. The time had dragged, and yet it seemed to have moved so fast. But then a lot had happened. The party must have been going for a long time before Carl and Helen had arrived.

She wondered how much time they had left.

That was it! she realized, looking nervously at the fireplace. *Time had seemed to go by because of the fear that these might be her last moments. Her last day on earth!*

That thought stopped her. She couldn't die. It couldn't end like this. Fury laced through her body like fire. This couldn't be her last day! Not if she had anything to say about it! Not by a long shot. If she was going to be killed, regardless, it might as well be in an attempt at getting free from these killers.

She looked over toward Helen again. The woman was staring at the bedroom door, her eyes slightly glassy, but deeply filled with apparent confusion. It wouldn't be too long before the woman broke under the tension, Pat realized. Or was that simply a desperate hope. Maybe a little more shoving might help.

"How long does he take?" Pat asked in a cutting voice. "She must be enjoying it!"

"Sure...I bet she is!" Helen snapped. "He's good, my man is!"

"And that doesn't bother you? I can't believe it!" Pat announce, rather brazenly. "I don't think you'd like that at all!"

Helen didn't say anything, but instead she took another drink of the whiskey in her hands.

That was good. Get drunk, and then it will be easier to get the gun away from you!

Pat started to rise, speaking very fast: "What do you think he's doing in there? Kissing her? Caressing her? Making love to her and all the time comparing you to her? Do you think he likes her better? Do you sit and wonder that maybe he will decide to throw you over for her?"

"Oh! Shut up!" Helen snapped, standing and looking violently at Pat. "Shut your damned slutty mouth!"

"Can't you take it?" Pat challenged. "Rena's quite a woman, I've been told."

The gun leveled at Pat's stomach and Helen's face went white with fury. "I'll kill you if you say another word. And don't think I am fooling!"

Pat felt it was a bluff, but decided not to call it—not yet, anyway. There might be time in a little while to bring it to a head—before Carl came strutting out of the bedroom.

"What's with you?" Helen asked. "Don't you know he's just raping her?"

The word rape seemed out of place when applied to Rena even to Pat. Rena wasn't the type of woman who would really hate the idea of forced seduction; once the right buttons had been pushed, Rena would surely respond.

"He's forcing her!" Helen continued. "Why should I care about that? I ask you, why?"

"Then why are you?" Gene asked, breaking into the conversation.

"I'm not! I don't care. Not in the least!"

There was a silence to answer that last remark, because nobody really believed her. The words had not only been illogical, but her tone of voice had lacked all sound of conviction.

"Why should I care?" Helen asked, glancing at the bedroom door. "He's just having a little fun—that's all. Just a little fun with a fat little tramp!"

132

Nobody said anything. There wasn't anything necessary to say. Helen was doing all the talking. She seemed to be getting herself into the state of mind that Pat had hoped to push her into.

Pat smiled and turned to the almost dead fireplace.

It wouldn't be long now, she thought, looking down at the coals. *It wouldn't be long until Helen really blew up all over the place. And that would give them their chance— and maybe* only *chance.*

Suddenly the bedroom door opened and Carl walked into the room.

"What a wild shot that slut gives!" he exclaimed, grinning from ear to ear.

Helen jerked around toward Carl, a look of confusion blanching her face.

"She's really a knocker!" Carl continued, stepping to the bar and pouring himself a drink. "A real hot chili pet! What a pleasure! I'd like to keep her as a life long pet to pet!"

"Just what do you mean by that!" Helen demanded, her face beginning to distort with rage.

Carl looked at her, and then smiled. "What do you think, baby?" he asked, sneeringly. "That she's so good a souped up lay that I couldn't get me enough of her hot body. And she likes it as much as you do! Heck, maybe even better than that!"

"And where does that put me?" Helen wanted to know. Her hand, which was holding the gun, slowly was raising, and Carl didn't miss the implication.

"Don't be silly," he said, moving up to her and taking the gun from her tight fingers. "You're the only girl for me!" He put an affectionate arm around her. "What's gotten into you?"

"Well..." her voice was unsure of itself.

"Come on—you know better than that!"

"They said that you might be—" She broke off suddenly, turning and looking evilly toward Pat. "She's the one that's been saying things!"

Carl's face gained a knowing expression. "Trying to turn her against me? Trying to make trouble for me?" His

133

expression turned to rage and he took a step toward Pat. "You making trouble for me with my woman?"

"Wait!" Helen cried. "Let me handle it!" Her voice was heavy with anger and hate. "Let me take care of this little bitch so that nobody will look at her lovely face again—so that she doesn't ever have a pretty face again!"

XXIV.

FOOL'S PLAY

The two detectives who were assigned to cover the mountain lake resort received a call from headquarters.

"Got something interesting for you guys. This Anderson guy has a brother who has a cabin up at the lake. If he's anywhere he will probably be there."

That was all the information they needed. Now they had to only wait until it was possible to get to the cabin—until the roads could be cleared. The storm had stopped and the snow had stopped. Just a short wait until the roads were cleared and then it would only be a matter of time...

Assuming that a copter couldn't be brought into action. But that didn't seem necessary at this point, so they didn't call in for one. If they could not get it then Carl Anderson couldn't get out.

* * * * * * *

Rena lay on the bed for a long time trying to think out her reactions to what had just taken place. She hated Carl Anderson, body and soul.

It was one thing to be taken to bed with any respectable guy for a good party. She liked that and always had. Her powerful need for sex had driven her to all means of getting what her body craved so badly.

But this was something different. This was raw and disgusting. It was forced seduction and she didn't like it. It was different from being picked up—willingly. It was, of course, rape.

Only Rena found that idea somewhat confusing.

And what she hated most about the whole thing was how much her body had liked it; her body had quickly responded to the caresses and kisses and the rough muscular form of Carl Anderson. The man was a savage, yet stunningly skilled.

He was good-looking—the kind of man she would have gone out of her way to pick up. The kind of hard, lean body that she had always favored in a man.

And rape or not, she had liked it so damned much—her body had responded all on its own, savagely thrilling to every damning act. It was like an alcoholic being forced to drink and in an instant gulping hungrily on the liquor. Her body had no morality; no sense of right or wrong—it only hungered. She had always been that way. She basically couldn't get enough. She had simply considered herself a free spirited woman, willing to enjoy life to the fullest.

But the way she had enjoyed Carl Anderson, despite herself, was disgusting.

One part of her wanted to vomit, as he had closed the door behind him, leaving her alone to deal with the aftermath of their long session on the bed together.

That was what made her so sick inside; sick to think that even when her mind was revolted, her body craved more.

He had started caressing and touching her, and oh, how she had responded. Every nerve just went into hot flashing overdrive. He pushed the right buttons and her body had gone at automatic tilt!

That's what made her hate herself.

What kind of animal was she?

In those first moments when he fairly yanked her head down to his groin, demanding her kisses, she'd simply gone out of control, without thought. He simply became male body parts, without any personality or identity other than an amazing skill and endurance.

A shiver of disgust now moved across her body. Hate clouded her mind, and she felt such an overwhelming emotion twist in her insides that it left her dizzy.

That was only the beginning. The man was amazing! With any other guy it would have been wonderful. And he keep at her, laughing against her breasts, body, tongue, hands and fingers discovering every trigger in her—causing her to gasp in shocked pleasure, thrashing on the bed, ripping at the sheets, then clawing at his arms and back, clawing at him as her lips were moaning in delicious pleasure. She wanted to scream in the utter ecstasy of his savage body fairly devouring her flesh and driving at her at every point he could get to. She was overwhelmed by the continued demands he kept making, again and again surging one place after another, changing, shifting, hands stroking her at one moment, then the delicious power of him penetrating so deep it made her gasp, almost choking, gagging as her body buckled and shuttered. Then suddenly he was unhurriedly moving with her, in an amazing unified rhythm. All at once they skillfully matched one another's actions. It was a deliciously slow dance that brought wave upon wave of ecstasy over her mind and body. It was like being drown in a heavenly drunken bliss. She was once again murmuring, purring, moaning, and clutching the man tighter and tighter in her arms, then gripping him with her thighs in fear he'd slip away before she'd been totally sated with the need he kept spinning through her with every move. At moments he seemed to just play teasingly with her, amused by her desperate need for more.

At one point he said in open admiration: "You...can't get enough!"

She shivered, wantonly in very real need.

"Tell me. Say it, baby!" he said, cruelly lifting away. "Say what you want!"

Her eyes popped open. She looked up at his cold face.

"Say it, if you want more...!" He teased her with a slight downward motion and she arched, moaning with want. "Say it!"

Again she experienced the horrid tease of him.

"Please..." she moaned, totally out of control.

Laughter came soft and brutal as he rammed down into her.

Rena didn't know how long it had lasted after that, but it did continue, and she couldn't stop her body from responding to that horrid man's continual assault.

Now, exhausted, laying on her back, where he'd left her, she wanted to cry, shame shivering every nerve. She wanted to die knowing how his rape had exposed her for an uncontrolled animal.

I have no class, she thought, sick. *Maybe I never did. Maybe dad was right about me.*

But it was her body which had gone out of control.

Certainly not her mind, Rena tried to tell herself.

Yet it was all a part of the same thing. Body and mind were interlocked in such a tight, tangled web that it was impossible to really know where one started and the other ended.

Carl Anderson, more than anybody, had illustrated how totally her body was master of itself, and her mind was helpless in its uncontrollable grip.

Somehow she was going to make Carl Anderson pay for what he had just done to her! Not the rape part—but making her like it so damned much! That was what got her; that was what made her almost insane with hate.

Rena's face tensed white; her expression was stiff and hard as she slowly stood from the bed and started to get dressed. The bra clamped around her breasts; the panties slid up to her hips; then her dress arranged itself around her voluptuous form, hugging tight.

Looking in the mirror, Rena started making up her face, and then after a few moments, moved to the door. She opened it in time to hear Helen's voice cry: *"Let me take care of this little bitch so that nobody will look at her lovely face again—so that she doesn't ever have a pretty face again!"*

* * * * * * *

Gene stood there, looking from Carl to Helen and then to Pat. No one had moved after Helen's hate filled threat. They were too stunned to really believe what they heard. The sudden outburst had been much too explosive.

138

They didn't even notice when Rena entered the room.

Gene found it impossible to believe she could really mean what she was saying. Why would a woman want to cut up another's face?

Then he was forced to believe it when he heard Carl's voice laughingly say: "Go ahead! Have fun! Why not let you girls have a little fun!"

Then Helen moved forward, threateningly, to Pat.

That's when Gene moved into action. He jumped forward, between the two girls. "Come on, ladies—just calm down!"

Helen looked at him, hate flared in her eyes.

"Move!" she demanded in slowly spaced words. "Out of the way!"

"Calm down!" Gene countered.

"Keep out of it!" Carl's voice cried from behind him. "Just keep out of it!"

Gene looked in the man's direction and saw the gun pointing at his back.

"You can't let this go on!" Gene almost pleaded.

"Why not? She deserves anything that's coming to her! Trying to make trouble between Helen and myself—because of that slut I just screwed!"

Just then Rena leaped at Carl, clawing at his face from behind.

"What the—hell!" he cursed, attempting to detach the woman from him.

Gene and Noel moved as one trying to help Rena. Here was their big break. Maybe the only one. Their chance to finally disarm Carl.

But they had underestimated the man. With one powerful twist he threw Rena to the floor. His gun leveled toward Gene and Noel.

"Just stay where you are, my friends!" he growled, while swinging a savage kick toward Rena's body.

Gene couldn't believe what he was seeing. It didn't seem possible that anybody could be so sadistic!

Carl's foot connected at the pit of Rena's stomach, knocking her backwards. A terrified moan exploded from her agonized lips.

139

Then he kicked again, this time in her groin. Gene stepped forward, instinctively, not thinking about the pistol in Carl's hand.

There was the sound of a gun shot. That was the only thing that Gene was aware of at first. Then the burn in his shoulder. He felt himself being whipped around, while at the same time pushed backwards. His vision blurred and then refocused in time to see Carl's foot kick out at Rena for the third time, smashing into her ribs.

She lay silent, her eyes closed, her face relaxed. Then Carl slashed his foot across her face, ripping the nose to a bloody thing that had no shape.

"That'll teach the bitch! Nobody does that to Carl Anderson and gets away with it."

The man didn't even look at Gene. He was only interested in examining in detail the damage that he had done to Rena's face.

He chuckled, satisfied that she was really damaged.

Gene felt sick, and he didn't think that it was caused by the burn in his shoulder. Suddenly the world started whirling and spinning downwards, sucking him into a blackness that lacked all shape and all sound and all awareness of the real world. All he knew was that he was floating in a dark sea and nothing was bothering him.

* * * * * * *

Pat felt a scream choke in her throat as she saw the gun go off, and she watched Gene as he was jerked backwards several feet. Her fear of the threat that Helen had made hadn't been anything—for some reason she'd been only numbed. But when Gene was shot, without any warning, she felt sickness rush through her. Even the brutal, unreasonable beating of Rena hadn't really caused any reaction in her.

Hurriedly, she rushed to Gene's side and took hold of his head. Tears welled in her eyes as she tried to see how bad the wound was. But it didn't do any good to look—at first— because her vision was too blurred.

Finally she wiped her eyes and then after blinking several times found it possible to examine the bloody smear

140

under Gene's jacket. The bullet had struck his shoulder, only grazing the flesh. Relief sighed through her, and almost at the same time Gene stirred and opened his eyes. For a moment he looked up at her and then smiled quite crookedly.

"You're okay!" Pat told him. "Just a flesh." She tried to smile, but the effort was only a thin muscular movement of her lips; she felt more like crying.

Gene tried to sit up and she helped him. Neither of them seemed to be interested in what was going on around them in the room.

It seemed to Pat that they were really alone.

And in a way this was true, for they had enclosed themselves in a world of their own. For the first time in weeks they were close, touching and not fearful of showing how they felt.

Maybe it was too late for either of them; she didn't know—and it didn't really seem to matter any more. The important thing was that they were finally through the thin wall of false pride and acting like themselves; they were being what they most desired—in love, and not afraid.

"Are you—okay?" she asked, finally looking down at the red shoulder.

"I think so. Stunned me—what he did to Rena!"

Neither of them noticed Carl standing right next to them, looking and silently listening to what they were saying.

ANY ONE CAN DIE! BY CHARLES NUETZEL

142

XXV.

TERROR RULES

Carl Anderson's voice broke into their conversation, stunning them to silence and bringing them back to the real world in which they were held in the terror grip of a madman. "Just why should that bother you, hero-man? I see you got your own designs…on this lady. Why bother with the little slut over there?"

Gene started to respond, but the pressure of Pat's fingers on his arm caused him to choke down the words that would have merely fired unnecessary sparks between him and this horrid man.

Carl stared down at him for a long moment, as if he was trying to hold back some personal fury, and then finally he opened his mouth.

"Remember, Mister Gene boy," he said in an overly pleasant voice, "I do have the gun! Don't you forget that point. And that makes me a very big man! When I tell you to jump you jump very high, and when I tell you to die—you'll simply die!" Hate flared up in the man's eyes. "See what I mean?"

Gene didn't reply to that. He turned his attention to Pat, ignoring the gunman.

"Help me up, will you?" he asked.

For a moment the two of them struggled and then finally he was standing.

"Mind if I have a drink?" he asked Noel, without looking in Carl's direction.

Noel nodded and Gene started moving toward the bar. Carl's voice brought him to a halt. "I think you better ask the man in charge! Me!"

Gene ignored him and continued on his way toward the bar. He was reaching for the bottle of whiskey when Carl's hand gripped his shoulder and whipped him around. "I said to ask me, first!"

Gene looked coldly into the other's eyes, blinking. "I don't believe this is your place!"

The fingers gripped his shoulder tightened. "But I have the gun. Remember? And it is my place, too, by the way. But no matter!"

Carl suddenly rammed the barrel into Gene's stomach. The blow was so sudden and unexpected that the wind was completely smashed out of his lungs. Gene doubled over in agony. It took several seconds to gasp back some breath and by the time he had slightly recovered from the effects a new awareness had pushed through his consciousness. Suddenly he didn't care about anything but getting even with this man; not for himself but for Ray and Rena.

He looked toward where Rena was lying on the floor still unconscious. For some reason nobody had gone over to her; maybe because so many things were happening—too many things at once.

He needed that drink. Looking at Carl who was glaring at him with squinting eyes, Gene decided that there was only one possible way to get the man off guard, and that wasn't by fighting or arguing with him. He had the gun and wasn't afraid to use it as either a club or a killing weapon. Arguing got only one effect from the man, a beating or a killing.

"Okay," Gene finally said, trying to make his voice sound scared. "*Please* can I have a drink?"

Carl looked at him for just a second and then whipped out his free hand, slapping it across Gene's face. The blow jerked Gene's head to one side, but he didn't do anything but take it silently. Make Carl think that he was scared to death of him and there was a possible chance of getting him unawares. And that would be the only chance that any of them would have to get out of the mess alive.

144

And that was the only important thing. Get out and live.

Especially now that he knew how Pat felt: she loved him!

What a dirty shame it was. They had their chance and had blown it but good. It was a dirty damned shame!

All these thoughts were rushing through his mind as Carl continued to silently examine him. Finally the man's face split into a broad grin. "Okay, rummy, why not? Why not let the scared kid have a belt of booze or two? Blow a big one—because it might be your last. I don't want it said that Carl Anderson was a cruel bastard and didn't give a condemned man a last wish."

Noel stepped forward. "You're not really planning on killing..."

"Oh, shut up!" Carl looked meaningfully at his brother, then added, warningly: "Don't you bet on that. Don't you bet a goddamned penny!"

He was silent for a moment and then looked around the room at the others. "What reason would I have to let you all live? What reason? Convince me. Why?"

Helen looked at him, her mouth open wide.

"You gotta stop the killing, Carl. Be reasonable!" she sighed, her eyes widening just a little.

He stared at her. "What do you mean? Why not? I don't want nobody to know what I plan on doing. If I let them live they'll blab it all to the police—just like I told you before! What do you think this is? A game we're playing? You know what the score is! You of all people! You planned the whole thing. The robbery. Everything."

"Everything, but killing. *You* did that!" Helen snapped, turning her eyes viciously at him. "*That* I didn't have anything to do with!"

There was a silence as Carl stared at the woman, almost as if she were an odd stranger hard to understand. His breathing had shortened and his eyes narrowed. Finally he took a step in her direction. "What you think you are? You're in this just as deep as I am. Just as deep. And don't you forget it!"

Gene had stood there looking at the scene for a long time, actually unaware of how Carl's attention was so com-

pletely directed away from everyone in the room except
Helen. This would have been the time to strike; it would
have been the time to make his play. But he was paying too
much attention to what was being said to be aware of anything else. And then suddenly Carl's attention turned to the
others again, and the chance had passed them by.

Gene's attention once more turned to the still form of
Rena. Why didn't somebody do something about her? He
started toward the unconscious woman. As he moved, Pat
started to follow.

Gently, Gene leaned over, biting his lip against the
pain in his shoulder. He'd almost forgotten about the wound.
Something would have to be done about it. It might only be a
scratch, but it would have to be cleaned.

He examined Rena's bruised and battered body. Her
face was completely mutilated out of shape, blood-caked and
broken. But she was breathing.

"Help me, someone!" Gene called.

Noel was beside him in a second.

"Leave her alone!" Carl demanded. Both Gene and
Noel turned in shock.

"Leave her alone!"

"You must be kidding," Noel exploded angrily.

"Why?"

"She needs help!"

"Leave her where she is!" Carl told them again,
pointing the gun at them. "No one touches her. She got
what's coming to her—so leave her be!"

Gene felt anger flood up through him but forced himself to hold it down. Not now. Hold it back until the right
time.

But what could he do with a bad shoulder? He
couldn't fight and he couldn't get Noel aside and tell him of
his plans.

Yet, maybe Noel had some plans of his own.

"Mind if I clean my arm?"

"Yeah! You deserved what you got, too. So suffer a
bit!"

Shrugging painfully, Gene stepped over to the sofa
and sat down to wait.

146

Wait for what? Death or a chance to overpower an insane man with a gun?

ANY ONE CAN DIE! BY CHARLES NUETZEL

ACT SEVEN

ANY ONE CAN DIE! BY CHARLES NUETZEL

150

XXVI.

DRAGNET

The two detectives had waited until the roads had been cleared and then climbed into their police car and started up the mountain road. It would only be a few minutes before they arrived at the cabin of Noel Anderson.

The one not driving checked his gun and then put it back in the shoulder holster.

They drove in silence, grim-faced.

They knew that if they hit the jackpot and Carl Anderson was at the cabin there would be a gun fight and one of them might be killed. The thought of facing death was an everyday fact of life hanging over their lives, but neither of them embraced the idea. They had a duty to do and that was all there could be to it. If in the line of duty they were killed—well, that was the bad breaks. But regardless of everything else, they knew that this time they were about to face a desperate killer who had nothing to lose by killing them— or killing anybody for that matter. But they were professionals. Both of them had joined the force to serve, now they had a chance to prove how far it was possible to go in that service.

This wasn't a game; it was a matter of bringing in a killer, dead or alive.

Finally they came to the turnoff which was supposed to lead to the Anderson mountain cabin.

Less than a mile lay between them and the killer they sought, if that's where he was hiding.

* * * * * * *

It must have been more than an hour that Rena lay on the floor, still and quiet, hardly seeming to breathe.

Nobody had said much during that time. It was as if all were waiting for something to happen, but weren't quite sure what it was they expected to take place.

Pat didn't want to die. Nor did the others.

The silence was heavy and hot.

The storm had stopped hours before but the air still felt like another storm was about to break—one of a different kind.

What did Carl Anderson really plan on doing to them? Line them along the wall and then shoot each in turn?

When was he going to kill them?

The helplessness of the situation was overwhelming.

The tension was becoming a tight knob of fear that looped through every corner of the room like a live wire. And there seemed to be no escape, no way to get out, and no way to stop the killing. They were like condemned criminals without any chance of a pardon. They waited for the killer to make his move

Then there was a knock on the front door.

Carl stood and pulled Helen upright. "Look, say nothing!" he ordered, moving toward Pat. "You come with me!"

The knocking continued.

Carl turned to Noel, whispering. "Answer it when we're in the bedroom—but one word and this little lady gets it first!" he announced, pointing his gun in Pat's direction. "Got me?"

Then he glanced at Rene's still unmoving form. "Dump the broad!"

He motioned the two men. "Move her into the kitchen!"

As they did so, he said to Helen: "Watch 'em, babe! Don't let them bring nothing dangerous back with them. A kitchen can be a dangerous place for—"

It all took a few minutes, while the knocking paused,

152

then continued on the door.

"Be right there," Noel shouted at the door.

Helen monitored the two men as they lifted Rena and half carried her into the kitchen. She held the door open, watching to see they didn't try to take anything out of the room.

Pat felt Carl's hand grip painfully on her arm and then half drag her across the room and into the bedroom as Helen joined them.

The knocking continued.

"Be right there!" Noel shouted again, from the kitchen.

"You just keep a closed lip and you won't get hurt any!" Carl told Pat, whipping her around behind him and sliding close to the all-but-closed door. There was a small crack through which he could see. "Keep an eye on her, Helen!"

Pat felt coldness inside her. Terrible fear was freezing in her guts and she couldn't get the feeling to leave.

* * * * * * *

When Noel opened the door, finally, there was an edge of tension in the room. Gene could feel all the nervous strain and terror gathering together for one gigantic explosion.

Two men were standing at the doorway.

"Can we came in?" one asked. Neither waited for an invitation. A moment later the door was closed behind them.

"Who's Noel Anderson?" The speaker asked.

"I'm Noel. And might I ask who you are?"

There was a tense silence and then the other man, the silent one of the newcomers, reached into his jacket and his hand came out with a gun.

"We're from the police—looking for your brother." His eye had snapped toward the bedroom door, seeing it open a crack. "We have reason to believe that he may be here at the—" As he had been speaking, his gun had raised toward the door. He broke off abruptly and then said: "Who's ever in there, come on out!"

153

The door swung open and Carl made two quick movements. His first bullet smashed into the side of the first armed detective, whipping him around and smashing him to the door. The other detective already had his gun out and was aiming it at Carl.

The second and third shots exploded at the same time. One just missed the detective and the second splattered into the door frame next to Carl.

Carl leaped back into cover and closed the door behind him. They heard his voice. "I got a lady in here with me—you stay where you are, or I'll kill her!"

That stopped the detective from moving forward. The man looked toward June, Noel and Gene.

"Is that true?"

Gene nodded. "And he'll kill her—that's for sure."

Strangely there was no sound from the other room.

Gene moved to the dead detective. Bending over, he saw the gun next to man's body. He just shook his head from side to side toward the other detective. Then, picking up the gun from the floor where it had fallen, he gripped it in his right hand.

Everything was blanketed in silence.

The officer noted what he'd done, shook his head, "This is a police matter..."

"That's my woman they have in there!" Gene retorted very soft and quickly.

There was a lingering silence for a moment.

Then Noel asked: "What do we do now?"

They all turned towards the bedroom door behind which the other three should be waiting. What was making them so quite?

Then suddenly a rustling sounded, a sliding noise whispered through the closed door.

"Is there a way out of that room?" the detective asked.

Noel shook his head. "Just the window. That's—"

His voice was brought to an abrupt stop by the sound of a car engine starting.

The detective and Gene both looked in the direction of the sound—outside.

154

Quickly they swung the front door open just in time to see one of the three cars which had been parked outside puffing away.

Carl and the two women were in it.

ANY <u>ONE</u> CAN DIE! BY CHARLES NUETZEL

XXVII.

ESCAPE ROUTE FINAL

The moment Carl had fired and then backed into the bedroom again he began looking for a means of escape. The window caught his eye.

"Okay, you two—follow me!" he commanded in a thin whisper. "And one word and you're dead," he told Pat.

The three of them stepped out of the window into the snow and silently moved around the cabin and into Carl's car which was parked outside.

Helen got behind the wheel and started the engine.

"Pull away fast!" Carl demanded, looking around at the cabin, his eyes alert for any movement in that direction. "Hurry."

They were pulling away when the cabin door opened and the detective and Gene rushed out. Carl pointed his gun out the window and fired a couple of shots in that direction.

"Step on it. They'll be on our trail in moments..." His voice trailed off and his mind burned furiously. "Damn it all—everything's gone to rot. I should have killed them all right off and this wouldn't have happened!"

Helen didn't say anything and Pat just sat frozen and unmoving.

The car went down the mountain as fast as Helen was able to drive it on the slippery road. The tires skidded and the car edged dangerously toward the end of the mountainside.

"Be careful!" Carl cursed, glancing back over his shoulder to see if there was any car following them yet.

157

"When you get into the resort area turn left; from there we'll go through the mountains and out across the state line, once there they won't be able to get me. I'll be safe for a while. In the meantime, if anybody gets too close; this little woman here will be good insurance. Very good insurance, indeed."

Pat spoke for the first time. "Once you're safe? What then?"

An evil grin spread across Carl's features, giving them the look of some demon from the lowest rotting pits of hell. "Well now, who knows? You might be good sport. Very good sport—more classy than that tramp. But, oh, man was she something!" He laughed at her shocked expression. "Honey, I think I could make you sing Yankee Doodle me some more! But you'll whimper to get more of me! Right honey?"

That last was offered to Helen, who simply laughed. "He's a tricky dickey, he is!"

"I sure am. And that lady back there couldn't get enough of it!" He hollered in delight. "And moaned and groaned like a whipped puppy. I do that to a lady, don't I?"

"You sure do, Carl, baby!" she quickly agreed. "You drive a lady wild, you do!"

"I sure do! Don't I? Wonderful being out, free at last. Free to enjoy the wonders of a woman!" He studied Pat for a moment, then said more thoughtfully, "You don't look sluttish at all! What were you doing at that party?"

Without waiting for an answer he offered: "I met you had 'em all fooled. Bet you're one of those classy lady-doves who prance it cool and icy until they get in with a real man. Bet you're a hot number once you get in the right setting. Don't you think so, Helen?"

The other woman merely shrugged, paying full attention to the driving.

Carl reached out to touch Pat, but she drew back, horrified.

"See...I was right!" he laughed. "You're just a classy tramp who'll be more fun to discover. Might as well enjoy the pleasures...the more you please me, maybe the longer you'll live!"

Pat didn't really consider herself a prude, but she'd

158

rather die than have this animal even touch her.

The man saw her horrified expression and spat: "You best shape up—I can be very nasty, too! Some women don't like what I do to them…most just love me up a storm. It'll all depend on you're attitude when I take you in me arms." He laughed again, then added: "And it'll happen. Believe me! Before the day is up! And you'll scream in pain or ecstasy!"

She said: "First you have to get away."

"We will. Believe me. We will. Than you're gonna have a feast you never imagined possible!"

His laughter chilled down her spine like ice. Her mind simply curled in on itself, horrified at the idea of what he could do to people—to her.

Oh, God, help me, she silently prayed.

ANY ONE CAN DIE! BY CHARLES NUETZEL

XXVIII.

CHASE

Gene followed the detective into the squad car, as Noel and June hung back, at the cabin porch.

They didn't speak to each other as the officer started the engine. Then after a moment they were following the other car, but much slower.

"Can't you go faster?" Gene demanded.

The man just shook his head and reached for the car radio. "It won't be necessary. I'll have a few road blocks set up so that he can't get out of the mountain area without running into one hell of a lot of trouble."

It was only a matter of minutes to arrange matters over the police radio. "He can't go anyplace except into a nicely setup trap."

"What about Pat?"

The other man didn't say anything for a moment.

"What about her? Will she be safe?"

"We can only do our best. It's all up to what Carl Anderson does. In either case, if he escapes with her there's…"

"…little chance of her living," Gene finished for the other man, feeling hard ice tighten in his guts. His fingers felt the gun, examining it blindly. One thing he promised himself: *I'll kill Carl Anderson if the man does anything to Pat. I'll track the guy down and blow his goddamned dirty brains out!*

161

ANY ONE CAN DIE! BY CHARLES NUETZEL

* * * * * * *

Pat felt icy sweat moving over her body; it was fear and utter disgust. Dying was one thing—easier than dealing with what Carl had in store for her. If Carl managed to escape. And it seemed that was exactly what would happen.

They had driven through town and now were on their way up toward the state line which was supposed to be at least sixty or seventy miles away. From all indications there wasn't anybody following them; yet she was sure that Gene at least would have followed.

Carl kept looking back though hadn't spotted anybody behind them. But on the curving mountain road it was hard to see very far and there was no way of knowing for sure if somebody wasn't just around the next bend beyond their line of vision.

Then after what seemed several hours to Pat, they came to a long stretch where it was possible to see behind them for several miles. That's when Carl spotted the police car. It was only assumed that it was the police because of the speed it was traveling.

"Step on it!" he demanded of Helen as he started to reload his gun.

Sweat was showing on his face now and his hands were slightly shaky.

They rounded a curve and were suddenly faced by a road block.

Helen, instead of continuing right on through, slammed the brakes on, not thinking of anything except that there was a car blocking the road.

"Go around it!" Carl screamed angrily, while reaching out through the open window and firing at the policemen standing on the road.

The car swerved as a bullet hit the front left tire.

Helen tried desperately to control the wheel, while at the same time trying to bring the car to a stop.

Carl managed to keep his nerves calm enough to take aim at the policemen. He hit one of them at the same time that the car plowed into the police sedan.

Everything was deadly quiet after that. Pat had been

162

thrown forward, her head hitting the dashboard, stunning her. Blackness tried to take shape before her eyes and then finally she was able to struggle back to consciousness.

Slowly she sat up. Her head hurt in a numbed sort of way, but otherwise she didn't seem to be hurt much. She was just about to turn toward Carl Anderson when she felt his rough hand grab her arm.

"Come on, baby!" he ordered.

She was dragged from the car and then pushed forward. "We got a little walking to do."

Pat suddenly noticed Helen wasn't with them. Then she looked toward the car. The woman was lying on the back of the front seat. There was a smear of red splashed across her face with a dark jagged hole centering on top of the bloody crimson.

"The cops hit her!" was Carl's only statement. He started to push Pat forward and then pulled her to a stop.

"No—I got a better plan—a much better one!"

ANY ONE CAN DIE! BY CHARLES NUETZEL

XXIX.

LAST STAND

The detective brought the car to a stop in front of the wreck at the road block. "What the hell!"

Gene felt a tightening in his throat. *Pat, what had happened to her?*

Both of them leaped from the car without saying another word.

They hadn't gone five steps before there was a voice calling out to them. "Just stay where you are!"

It was Carl Anderson.

Gene tensed. The gun in his hand was half hidden against his leg and he made it a point to keep it hidden. It was an ace in the hole.

Carl Anderson stepped out from behind the wrecked police car and moved toward them. In front of the convict was Pat, white-faced and afraid. Her lips were thin pale lines, her eyes wide.

"Don't be a hero, copper, or this girl gets it good!" Carl demanded, moving forward slowly, his gun pointing at the detective.

The two of them froze, not moving.

Carl started toward the car, moving slowly, keeping his eyes on the other two men.

"Leave the girl here," Gene said.

"You giving orders, buddy?"

"Leave her here!"

"What for? I need her. She's my safeguard."

165

Gene felt a dry lump tighten in his throat and sweat pour down his body. "What good will it do to take her!"

Carl grinned evilly. "What do you think, hero-man? What do you think a woman is good for—for a real man?"

Pat tensed; fear clouded her features, tighter this time.

Just at that same moment Carl's eyes were on the detective and the angle of his body was such that it was possible for a clean shot from Gene's gun. The only thing was that he wasn't sure he could take a chance. He'd been good with a rifle at one time, but with a pistol it was something else.

Pat caught the action of his hand as he brought the gun up level with what he hoped was Carl Anderson's body. At the same time he yelled: "Pat, drop!"

Then he fired as he saw the girl move from between them.

As he pulled the trigger, the detective reached under his jacket and his hand came out with a gun.

Carl fired once then twice at the police officer. Totally ignoring Gene.

A bullet entered the detective's body, sending him spinning.

Gene fired again.

A complete second miss.

Carl's gun aimed at Gene and just as he was pulling the trigger Pat raised upwards in an effort to yank his arm away from Gene's direction.

The explosion left a dead silence on the mountain scene.

Pat slowly slumped toward the ground. Carl looked puzzled at her and then moved his gun back up to Gene.

What had just happened drove sanity away. In a rage Gene started running forward, grief choking his throat. He didn't care if he died or not; his only desire was to take Carl Anderson with him. At closer range he was sure of hitting the gunman.

He was determined to kill the man for what he'd done to Pat. Kill him no matter what.

He fired as he ran, just pointing the gun like he would his index finger, squeezing the trigger.

166

His third bullet seared into the other's forearm and his fourth creased the man's head. But Carl remained standing, as if paralyzed, just pointing his gun at Gene. A look of shock on his face.

Gene fired again. There was a metallic click.

Carl's face creased in a broad victorious smile. "Well now, my little hero..."

The words halted as he saw that Gene was still coming. Then desperately, without aiming, he fired his gun.

The bullet burned into Gene's side but for some reason it didn't seem to bother him.

The hand that held the empty gun swung out at Carl's face, ripping across it and causing a bloody gash three inches long to expose raw flesh. Again his gun hand slammed at Carl. This time on the back of the head.

Without a sound the man fell to the ground, unconscious.

With blind anger Gene's foot smashed into the killer's stomach and then he heard a voice behind him.

"Stop it, man!"

He turned and saw the detective standing, weakly holding a bloody smear on his side. "You've done enough damage. His fangs are pulled. You best look after the woman. She's hurt bad."

That fact stunned him out of the insanity that had overtaken every thought. It was the first time that he even thought that Pat might not be dead. At the close range she had been shot it seemed impossible to believe she could have survived.

"She's alive?"

"Barely!" the detective announced, slipping behind the wheel of his squad car. "I'll have a copter here as soon as possible."

Gene ran toward the still form of Pat and bent over her. There was a crimson hole at her chest. Too close to the heart.

But she was still alive.

His first impulse was to cradle her in his arms, but then he realized that moving her might cause more damage.

Tears welled in his eyes and his heart beat faster.

167

ANY ONE CAN DIE! BY CHARLES NUETZEL

His mind screamed in painful desperation.
God, let her live! Let her live!

XXX.

EPILOGUE

It had been hours since the doctor had started work on Pat, and the hours seemed more like years to Gene who had been told to stay in the waiting room until there was word from the operation room.

Gene heard footsteps and jerked in the direction of the sound, expecting to see the doctor. His heart pounded and his guts tightened.

God! Don't let her be dead! his mind pleaded for the thousandth time.

Noel Anderson walked in. His face was drawn and tired.

"Hello," was his only greeting. Then, taking a deep breathe, he asked: "How is she—have you heard?"

"I—I don't know. The doctor said she was lucky to be alive. I'm waiting word."

Noel's eyes noticed that Gene's arm was in a sling. "I see they fixed you up."

"A couple of hours ago."

"Rena is okay, just banged up." Noel coughed nervously and then said: "I feel horrible about all this—I mean about Carl. He was always a terror, even as a kid. Don't know what went wrong. Crazy. I thought he was locked up for good. If I'd know… If I just hadn't come to the cabin or invited you folks over—"

"Forget it. Nobody could have known!"

If these events hadn't taken place he wouldn't have

169

Pat in his life. And she would not have been hurt—maybe killed. What irony! But there was nothing that could change what had happened. They all had to live with the past and make the most of what was in their future—assuming there would be one worth living.

Without Pat he simply didn't care.

So all that was left was to wait.

They fell into silence again, and neither of them spoke for more than an hour; they just sat smoking nervously and looking at the floor or the far wall.

Then a nurse walked in and asked: "Mr. Bates?"

She looked at each of them.

Gene stood up slowly, almost afraid to hear what might be following.

"Follow me," she told him without saying anything else. Gene breathed a sigh and looked at Noel for a second and then moved after the nurse.

They walked down a long corridor and passed several desks with nurses behind them; turned down another hallway and then finally came to a stop before a room whose door was closed.

There was a moment of silence and then the door opened and the doctor who had been working on Pat stepped out. He spotted Gene and his face turned slightly grim. For a moment he didn't say anything. Then finally his mouth opened.

Gene felt his heart beating faster and faster. Dread was racing through his whole body—he was afraid to hear what the doctor had to say.

"She's gone through quite a bit. Still unconscious—but she'll be coming out of it in a little while."

Then the doctor smiled, very tiredly. "Thought you might want to be here when she wakes."

He indicated the room. "Just be quiet and don't try to talk to her much."

The doctor said a few more things, but Gene wasn't listening. Only one thought was running through his tired mind now: *Pat was alive!*

For the first time in weeks he was glad to be alive, too. There was a happy future ahead. Marriage. Settling

170

down and having kids.

He stepped into the room and looked down at his future wife.

ABOUT THE AUTHOR

Charles Nuetzel was born in San Francisco in 1934, and writes:

"As long as I can remember I wanted to be a writer. It was a dream I never thought would materialize. But with the help of Forrest J Ackerman, who became my agent, I managed to finally make it into print.

"I was lucky enough not only in selling my work to publishers but also ending up packaging books for some of them, and finally becoming a 'publisher' much like those who had bought my first novels. From there it as a simple leap to editing not only a sci-fi anthology, but a line of sci-fi books for Powell Sci-Fi back in the 1960s. Throughout these active professional years I had the chance to design some covers and do graphic cover layouts for pocket books & magazines."

Much of his work in covers and graphics are a result of having had a father who was a professional commercial artist, and who did a number of covers for sci-fi magazines in the 1950s and later for pocket books—even for some of Mr. Nuetzel's books.

In retirement he has become involved in swing dancing, a long time lover of Big Band jazz. But more interestingly world travels have taken him (and his wife Brigitte) across the world, to Hawaii, Caribbean, Mexico, Kenya, Egypt, Peru, having a lifelong interest in ancient civilizations. His website is full of thousands of pictures taken during these trips.